G R JORDAN

Scarlett O'Meara: Beastmaster

SETAA Book 1

First edition

ISBN: 978-1-912153-35-0

Cover art by J Caleb Clarke
Editing by Roma Gray

This book was professionally typeset on Reedsy.
Find out more at reedsy.com

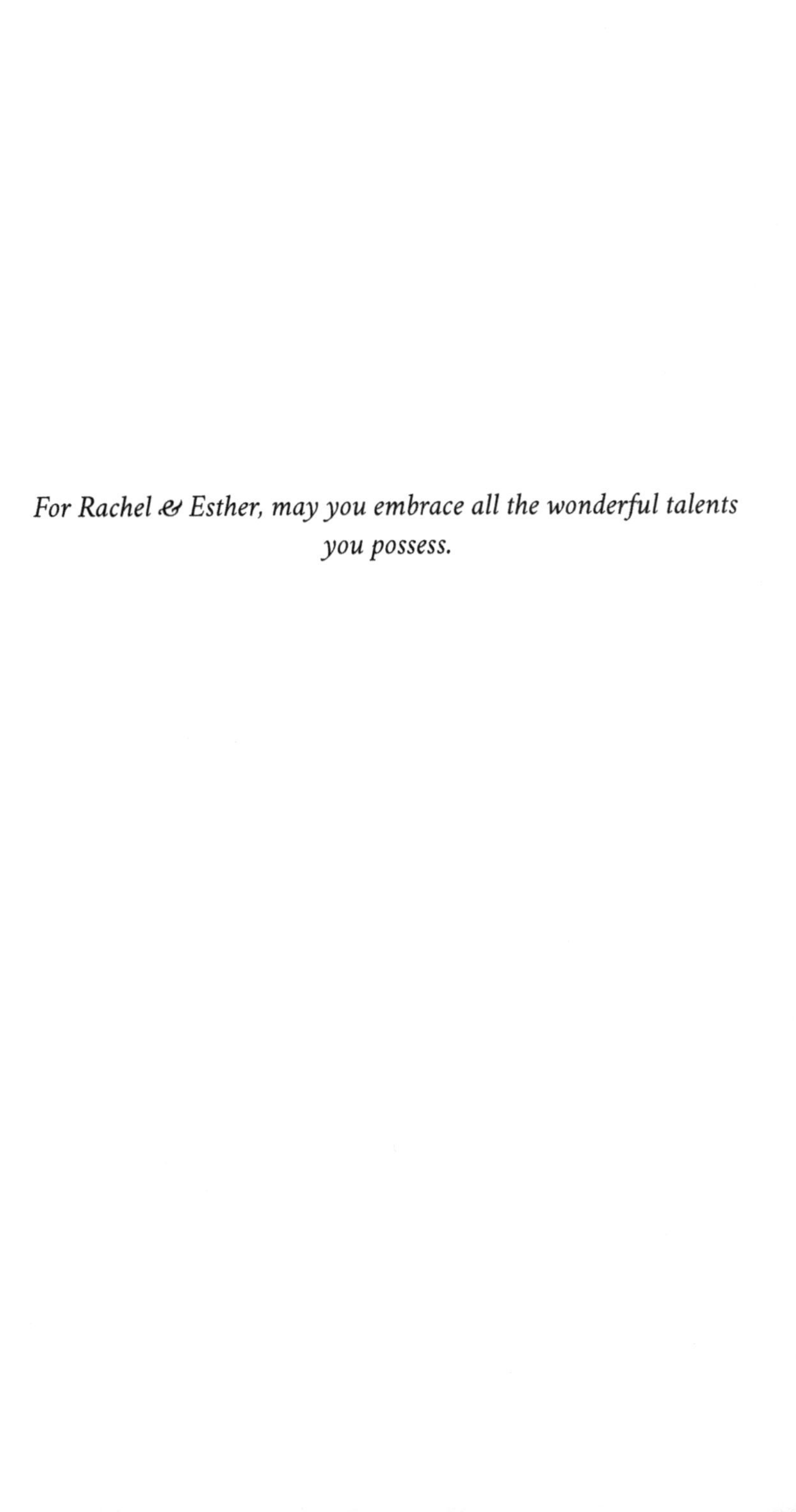

For Rachel & Esther, may you embrace all the wonderful talents you possess.

Contents

Acknowledgement

First to my Janet and my family who let this man with weird ideas and stories fill up his hours by tapping into a keyboard. They are the people who make life worthwhile.

To Roma for her patience on this tale and for helping break through the mess the initial drafts were.

To all the writers and readers who make producing books fun, your joy is my joy.

To the team at the station for making the days go quicker and the support when they didn't. You've helped me have moments to be proud of.

To God, for his guidance and for the gift of stories in this world. If we shared them more, then maybe we'd understand each other better.

1

Sought-After Body

The long night had been an unexpected one. As Scarlett splashed the water onto her face, she thought back to how the old soldier had bought her drink after drink until she couldn't remember them coming any more. It seemed to her that she was getting attention that she had never received from her previous boyfriend. Brendan, in some ways had been perfect, but in other ways, he hadn't seemed interested in her. She wondered if her own shortcomings were the problem: the way she looked, the way she talked with that uniquely Welsh accent, or her insistent chattering across the top of everything. The old soldier, on the other hand, seemed delighted with her constant yammering, indeed it seemed to be something that really appealed to him. *Whatever,* she thought. He was now just a memory, disappearing in a pile of other memories collected during her new "getaway" life that she felt compelled to undertake when Brendan dumped her.

Her tired eyes looked in the mirror where her face was somewhat paler than normal. Never again would she accept that many drinks. Turning to find some towels to wipe down her face, Scarlett arched her back, rubbed her face and then made for the exit. Her feet were slightly unsteady, not because she was still drunk, but because she was more hung over, and well, feeling very delicate today.

She exited the restroom and was clattered into by a fast-moving person. It was a gentleman's frame much bigger than hers, and Scarlett felt her head smack into the cold floor beneath. The gentlemen landed on top, breathing heavily, obviously sweating. She tried to push him away, but he kept pushing down on her while his head was flicking from side to side apparently looking for someone. She felt a hand reach into her top and press upon her chest. *Bloody pervert.* And then he was up and away, running as if his life depended on it. If she had a say in the matter, it bloody well would.

A little groggy after the fall, Scarlett took a time getting back up. Before she could draw back up from the floor, she heard another set of footsteps run past her. Briefly, a face looked at her, then disappeared. It was deeply scarred on one side and gave a look like she didn't matter. *Be nice if some people these days would stop and help.* She managed to pick herself up off the ground, brushing down her skirt which was dusty from the floor. She readjusted her blouse, messed with her hair, giving her best efforts to get it back to normal before returning to her coach party which was sitting in the car park.

The driver patiently waited while she mounted the steps. As had been her habit throughout the trip, Scarlett took a seat at the front, barely glancing back down to note what she saw as the oldies and the desperate were doing while awaiting the next hotel. It was now evening, and it would be good to get to the next hotel, have a quick dinner, maybe a walk and then retire to bed. The effects of the previous night and the tumble were beginning to get to her.

The coach pulled away and re-entered the motorway, heading deep into the heart of Scotland. Scarlett nodded off and never saw the coach arrive at the next destination. A tap on the shoulder brought her back to consciousness, and she stepped off the bus and picked up her luggage. It was a small purple bag which was all she had managed to pack in the three hours between booking the trip and joining the coach. Yes, it was time for a shower and to wash away last night's escapades, keen to never do them again. She'd sort out this mess she'd become.

The hotel itself was typical of Middle Scotland. From outside the building, it looked rather grand in patches, but the issues of paintwork flaking, and curtains and drapes that looked rather drab compared to their previous splendour, killed the desired effect. An antiquated heating system failed to heat up the large bedrooms evocative of the period. *Oh well,* thought Scarlett, *let's hope the covers give a toasty effect to the unsturdy bed.* Toasty was always something she struggled for, always feeling cold wherever she was. *Although I was never cold when he was there,* she thought.

As she stood in the shower, letting the water flow over her body and wash away the day, Scarlett thought her life had turned into such a drab and boring mess. She never wanted to be a librarian. She wanted to explore, she wanted to go to far-off lands and find never before discovered creatures. She watched all the programs, saw all the magazine articles, talking about those cameramen away for days, weeks, sometimes years, to film the animals no one ever saw. Sometimes she thought that she could have done all this if only her mother had not insisted on a proper job, a proper job being a grocery assistant at the supermarket to bring money in on her 16th birthday. National qualifications, none whatsoever, apart from the fact she could stack shelves faster than anyone else. What was worse, was the fact she lived in a flat where she couldn't even have an animal for herself. There was a zoo only three miles from the building, and often she would get the bus and spend the day walking around from animal house to animal house, looking at the giraffes with their tall necks, sometimes listening to the belching of the hippos and other times watching the prairie dogs, their heads up and down looking out for danger. Animals she always seemed to connect with. Definitely better than with any person. Using the towel, she rubbed herself down and looked in a bag for something suitable for taking on a walk.

In the middle of February, the air was notoriously cool and crisp. The rain, having fallen mainly in the morning, gave way to weather that wasn't unpleasant but cool. Picking out some track bottoms, T-shirt and a large thick jumper, she picked a large coat which would wrap around her like some sort of duvet. With her trainers slipped on, she left the room and exited the hotel to the fresh air outside, hoping that the clear air would help her sore head and allow a good night sleep.

Stepping down the rather ornate steps at the front of the hotel, she strolled silently along the long driveway before reaching a small gate at the side of the main entrance. She was passing through this when several cars roared into the driveway, but although she saw them, they could not see her. They were black, official looking and had windows you couldn't see through. It was almost as if some celebrity was arriving, except that the cars looked much more official than that, maybe some sort of government minister?

When she had cleared the gate, she started off on a walk, her long blonde hair bobbing behind her in a swish pony tail. *Life needs to improve, life needs to get better, life needs to start,* she thought. Yes, she would need to get things together make her way in this world, forget the drab dreary things that she was doing. But inconsiderately, the road away from the hotel dipped sharply before rising again. This meant she had to walk up the hill, and Scarlett preferred flatter places, places where you didn't have to stretch your legs properly first, places where thighs didn't hurt when you walked (which always happened when she walked sharply downhill). Sometimes life just never sorted itself out.

The walk continued alongside fields where she could see the remnants of previous plantings, the fields not yet ready to take another dose of seed for the spring and summer ahead. She looked around, hearing the birds in the air, jealous of their ability to just fly anywhere, approach anywhere and sing anywhere. Singing was something else her mother had stopped her from doing. *Why, for goodness sake?* She was Welsh after all, she could actually sing.

After a short walk, she came upon a small forest, the entrance of which was at the side of the road. From what she could see ahead, it appeared to be just moors and this expanse of trees was the best piece of cover for the next few miles. Hearing the birds in the trees made her mind up and she decided to take a walk along the path.

The forest felt good. There was a smell in the air that you couldn't find anywhere else, a freshness.

Her mind unexpectedly returned to her stepmother back in the rest home. It was six months ago when she went into the rest home after the terrible fall that had left her paralyzed.

It was a godsend in some ways, as it got her stepmother off her back. During previous years, a girl from the state helped at the house, but now her mother was looked after by the state full-time. It sounded harsh when you put it like that, but she'd been tied down even when it came to boyfriends and mother interfered with everything. Now she was free. Free to get drunk with older men on a coach trip in the middle of nowhere. Yes, life would have to improve.

Scarlett wasn't even thirty yet. Life had been pretty well rubbish up to this point, but in the next year she would make thirty and she would be off doing things she wanted to do. She fully intended to visit her stepmother at the home from time to time, but no longer would the woman dominate her life, no longer would life be about doing for others, now it would be about getting a little for herself. And that did not include tagging up with people like Brendan. It was not that she was such an intellectual that she wanted every man to only dote on her mind. But it would be nice if they would draw their eyes from her chest for two minutes to have at least a moment. It wasn't like she was some sort of model either. At five foot three she was a bit stumpy. As one former boyfriend put it, "the product of a powerhouse and a prop forward to dream of." He didn't really know how to impress a lady.

Scarlett became aware that she wasn't alone. At first during her brisk walk she barely noticed the surroundings, having wandered down the path through the trees. But she now began to see and hear signs that seemed unusual. It was just a cracking of a twig, the sound of footsteps, almost as if someone was trying to alert her to their presence. Turning, she found a hand clamping over mouth, and she stared up into two eyes that said they wanted to do her harm. Almost immediately, the figure stepped around, his hand still across her mouth but now holding the rest of the body tight with his other arm. Scarlett wanted to scream but the grip was so tight she couldn't make a sound at all.

"Where is it, girl? Just tell me where it is."

Scarlett felt the hand release slightly, presumably to give an answer to the question. Instead, she screamed out loud.

"That's enough of that, you bitch."

The man roughly began to frisk her evidently searching for something. It was a bizarre feeling. Several times in darker moments, Scarlett had wondered how it would feel to be attacked. How would it feel to be at the mercy of a man stronger than herself? But this was nothing like she thought it would be like. And it soon became apparent that the man wasn't after her, after her body. He clearly wanted something she had but something that was buried on her.

"Hurry up! Ain't you searched her yet? Or are you having fun?"

It was a different voice. Not as deep as the first man but still clearly a man

"She doesn't seem to have it, doesn't know nothing."

Scarlett then heard one of the men gasp, followed by the sound of something heavy hitting the ground. The man holding her slightly loosened his grip, and Scarlett knew this was her chance. She drove a foot down hard on his. The man yelped and the grip was released slightly. It was enough for Scarlett to run forward in a desperate attempt to escape, but his hand latched onto her throat…but then suddenly she heard the man cry out. The hand released her, and he fell to his knees looking stunned. Scarlett didn't hesitate, launching a kick into the man's nether regions that would hopefully bring tears to his eyes. Beyond the man she saw face. A woman taller than herself, dressed in black leather from head to foot with long black hair. She was trim, obviously well used to a fight and had a grim look on her face.

"We need to go."

"I am not going with anyone," said Scarlett. "Just who the hell are you people?"

"Now isn't the time, you need to go. You need to come with me."

"Like I said, I'm not going!"

But the woman grabbed Scarlett's hand and dragged her back down the path she had come along earlier. She saw both men lying on the ground in pain but presumably they would be capable of moving again soon. It only took a few minutes to run back down the path to reach the roadside again where there were two vehicles. One was one of the black governmental type vehicles she had seen before and the other was a light blue transit van of which the door was now sliding open. It revealed a small man, the size of a child, standing in the doorway.

"Just get the car going, Rodriguez," said the woman. The man nodded and jumped through to the front seat while the woman threw Scarlett into the back before jumping inside, closing the door behind her.

"Go! Go! Go!" said the woman. The transit van roared and Scarlett rolled in the back of the van until she hit the doors at the back.

"You're lucky girl, you're damn lucky."

2

The Good Guys?

Scarlett felt around inside the van for anything that she could hold onto. It was careering along the road at a fast pace, and she was unsure of where she was going and who she was with. She was aware of the fact that the woman who had helped her into the van was watching her closely, only occasionally turning ahead to look at the window and see where they were going. The small man, who had been called Rodriguez, was driving the van but could not been seen over the height of the seat due to his own lack of height. Everything she was seeing was a blur at this time, and Scarlett was unsure of what was going on. All she knew was somebody had wanted something from her, and if these people hadn't turned up to help, well…, but she still didn't know who they were or why they were here.

"What did they want from you?" asked the woman. Her eyes were penetrating, her voice insistent but she did have a demeanour about her that said friend. Despite this, Scarlett wasn't going to trust anyone at face value and decided she probably shouldn't tell what happened during the last couple of hours.

"Who are you? What's happening to me?"

"We don't have time for this," said the woman in black, "what I need to know is what they were looking for? Where did they look on you?"

"I don't know what they are looking for, I haven't got anything. Who are you?" asked Scarlett again.

Are they still on us, Rodriguez?" the lady asked the man in the front.

"No, I think we've shaken them," said the small man in the front.

"Okay pull over, and we will see what our friend here knows."

Feeling the van pull to one side, Scarlett reckoned they disappeared along a track that sounded quite off-road. The van stopped, the engine going silent as the woman in black moved across the van. She reached out a hand to help Scarlett up into a sitting position. Her touch was cold, something akin to the inside of a fridge. Her skin was pale and rough, but other than that, she was extremely attractive. Her body, although cold, was obviously in shape, and she was a good couple of inches taller than Scarlett who always felt short at a mere five foot three. But for all that, Scarlett saw the woman was one of those girls who was always more athletically built but often thought of as less womanly. It was evident that Scarlett was using everything within her recesses to build herself up in the situation and she hoped that the woman was doing the same.

"The men that were after you were looking for something. Do you have it?" asked the woman in black.

"No, no, no!" said Scarlett. "Where do you get off asking these questions? I've been assaulted, I've been grabbed but you just ask me about some bloody object? I think the least you could do is ask 'Are you okay?'"

"Okay, are you okay?"

"I think so, thank you," retorted Scarlett.

"Good. Now may I know what they were looking and if they found it?" asked the woman in black again.

"No, no, no!" said Scarlett. "You tell me who you are first of all before I say anything to you."

"I am the woman who just came in here and saved your butt," retorted the woman in black, "but if you wanna call me something then it's Calandra and the man in front is Rodriguez, and we are here to help."

"It's funny that everyone always seems ready to help when they need something from you," said Scarlett. "Those people are looking for something from me, and I don't have anything."

Calandra looked at her quizzically before turning to Rodriguez. He was standing up on the seat looking over the top at both of them. There seemed to be a moment when they were sizing up each other's opinions before Calandra turned back.

"Has anything unusual happened, any moments in the last few hours that you thought were strange?"

"You mean apart from the attack just now, actually people constantly seem to be having a go at me." Calandra raised her eyebrows.

"Having a go? What and where and how?" she asked.

"Just that man who tried to grab something from inside my blouse, but it was like he was searching for something. It wasn't like he was trying to grab hold of things, so to speak," said Scarlett. "Not that that made it any better."

Calandra nodded. "Was there any other time when someone

tried to grab you in such a way? I mean recently."

"I was at a motorway services earlier on today," replied Scarlett, "and this man ran into me as I came out of the restrooms. He fell on top of me and reached down inside my blouse again but he was up and away. Before I could get up another man ran past me, desperately looking for the other man."

"And did he reach inside your blouse too?"

"No, not the second one but the first one, he wasn't acting like he was looking for something, more like he was almost placing something."

"Did he leave anything there? Was there anything left around your neck? Did he attach anything to you?" asked the woman in black.

"Not that I know of," said Scarlett.

The woman reached forward and grabbed Scarlett by the shoulders with one arm. She looked into her eyes. "Forgive me." Scarlett felt the hand of the woman drop inside her blouse and search around her breastbone. Again the touch was chilly, almost extreme but not to the point where her skin burned. After a few seconds of delving around the hand was removed.

"There's nothing there," said Calandra. "I need you to do me a favour, girl. Rodriguez turn your back a minute."

Rodriguez raised his eyebrows but turned and sat back down in his seat.

"Can you reach down inside? We need to see if anything is located in there. I think it is preferable you do it rather than me," said Calandra.

Scarlett looked suspicious at the bizarre request but the woman just nodded, her black hair delicately dancing round the edges of the face. Scarlett was worried that there was another option. If she didn't do it, it would no doubt be done for her.

"But if you don't mind," said Scarlett, "It would be better if neither of you was watching." The woman in black turned away leaving Scarlett happy that she would be the only one viewing. She reached down inside her underwear, searching for anything that might be there. She did find it odd to be subjected to looking for things in such a private area where surely things would be felt. After a few moments search it was evident there was nothing.

"There was nothing there. Nothing left, nothing given to me."

"But they must have left it on your person because they certainly believe it has been left with you," said Calandra, her face becoming more intense.

"I haven't got it! Now just drop me back at the hotel, I'll be on my way, and you can continue looking for whatever it is you need."

"I don't think you get it," said Calandra. "These people are looking for things from you. These people who believe you have something won't just turn up, ask for a quick search and disappear, because they think you *do* have it. They will take you, they will torture you until you give them what they think you have. And if you die before they can find it, it won't bother them one bit. They will search you to make sure you don't have it, just in case you didn't realise you had it, and then they'll dump your lifeless corpse by the side of the road. Is that what you want?"

Scarlett betrayed a worried face at the mention of death, but she was still confused. "What am I meant to have? What is it that is so important that I shouldn't have it?"

"I'm not totally sure. People I work for believe a certain artefact is missing. The said artefact is precious enough and dangerous enough that certain parties within this world will look to commandeer it. We believe it gives the bearer power over animals. Also over beasts a type of control. The groups that I work with, or against, can use this to gain an advantage, an advantage that might just tip the balance."

Scarlett's head was in a whirl. *What's this you've got into?* She looked down at her hands and they were trembling. The question she'd been asking previously seemed to drift away. The woman said they would torture her, the woman said they would kill her even if she didn't know anything. And yet she only just met this woman, albeit she had rescued her from those thugs.

"Rodriguez," said Calandra, "we need to get going back to this lady's hotel. We will need to search the rooms. If it's not on her, it must have been on some other part of the clothing." Calandra turned to Scarlett. "Are you wearing something different to what you were wearing earlier?"

Scarlett nodded. At the nod from Calandra, Rodriguez turned the engine on and Scarlett felt the van reversing back down the track they had driven into. She tried to lean back against the side of the van as it bounced along but it was uncomfortable as her head bounced off the side. She decided it was better to sit forward in a tense position. She looked up at the woman in black who was looking back at the scene, a smile on her face. Yet the worrying concern behind it was evident. *What am I into* thought Scarlett, *What is this?*

As the van drove along, presumably back to the hotel, Scarlett watched the woman in black open up a small trunk in the far corner of the van. From it she took what appeared to be a long stick. Carefully, she looked it over with her eyes and then touched the edge of it as if making sure something was working. She also removed two long knives from the trunk, fastened them to her person and tucked away a number of small objects, which appeared to be throwing items.

"Is that really necessary?" Asked Scarlett.

"Yes," said the woman in black, "very necessary. I don't believe you fully understand the people you're dealing with here. To be honest, I haven't been a minute with these people so I don't understand either. But you should see what Rodriguez packs."

This did nothing to allay Scarlett's fears. Looking out the front window of the van from her position at the rear, she could see trees passing by before recognising some of the scenery that was close to the hotel. Her stomach became a knot, and she remembered the governmental black cars she'd seen in on her way out. *Those people are already there, so how do we find anything? Surely the best thing to do would be to leave, get as far away as possible from the scene.*

"Calandra," said Scarlett, "what am I going to do? Do I just stay in the van while you two run off to look for my stuff, their stuff, whatever stuff is?"

"No," said Calandra, "you're coming with me. I can't afford to leave you here, not with all the people that are about. You wouldn't be able to protect yourself, and I have orders to above all else keep civilians protected."

"Civilians?" asked Scarlett.

"Yes, this is a war," Calandra said.

"Nearly there," called Rodriguez, "time to start looking frisky."

Scarlett had to reach for support as Rodriguez swung the

van. It screeched into the car park in front of the hotel, swung sideways, and Calandra was already opening the door to see what was beyond. Bizarrely, there was an eerie silence. Scarlett expected any number of shots and shapes of people running about, given Rodriguez's warning. But as Calandra stood at the door looking out there was nothing. No motion… It was as if they'd walked into the start of a horror movie, the low for the arrival of the monster. Scarlett watched Calandra's hand beckon her to move from the back of the van to sit beside Calandra. There was a sharp click clunk from the front of the van. Scarlett looked over and saw Rodriguez with the pump action shotgun raised to his face and aimed at the window. Scarlett swooned, feeling slightly faint. There was also something inside of that feeling which said she needed to keep going, that these people offered her the best protection. So she shuffled forward and took Calandra's cold and somewhat clammy hand.

As she stepped down from the van, Scarlett saw Calandra give the wooden stick she'd taken from the trunk a hard shake with her other hand. The stick expanded before her eyes until it was the height of Calandra herself, and Scarlett was amazed as she began to twirl it around the left hand only.

Looking back, Calandra commented, "It's not as good as my old one."

Scarlett stared forward across the open car park. Not once did Calandra look back at Scarlett but instead her eyes examined their surroundings, head turning all directions, scanning and then scanning some more. Rodriguez could be heard getting out of the van but was not seen. Scarlett knew the man was small, but surely she would have noticed him. As they approached the hotel entrance, it was obvious something was wrong. There were several panes of glass broken in the door, inside there was an eerie quiet. Over the reception desk was a body slumped face down on it with some redness dripped onto the sign-in book.

"I hope he's all right," said Scarlett.

"Silence," said Calandra. "Don't think, just do. Where's your room?"

"Upstairs," said Scarlett and pointed to the rather obvious staircase with its ornate wooden banister. Calandra glided along on her feet making no noise, Scarlett stuttering behind. They moved along the upper corridor towards Scarlett room which she occasionally had to point out the directions to. Other rooms were open, all the doors smashed to pieces. It seemed there had been some sort of a war going on inside the hotel, but this was all that remained afterwards. Scarlett turned her head away several times when she saw people who had been on the coach trip, people she didn't know well. Indeed, people she'd barely met but whose faces and bodies looked distinctly different to the way that she remembered. The things that Calandra had said about torture began to ring true in mind. She grasped Calandra's hand more tightly than she had before.

"Is this the room?" Asked Calandra.

"Yes," said Scarlett noting the number 15 on the front of the door. The door looked intact but was unusual as most of the others had some sort of significant damage on them at least if not totally destroyed. It was a surprise when Calandra simply lashed out with a left foot, kicking the door wide open. Inside, sitting in the chair by the bed, was a man. He had an eye patch across his left eye and scars on his face. The other immediately obvious thing was his left-hand, composed of metal. He stood and smiled a rather cheeky grin.

"Thank you for bringing her here as we've looked everywhere for the bitch."

3

Escape

Scarlett looked at the man in horror, eyes wide. Deep within, she felt her panic rise. She was aware that she was sweating profusely and her hands were clammy. Surely this woman, the saviour who had pulled her from the other men, had not brought her back to the people who were looking for her? This had been a mistake. Coming to her room may have led to her demise.

A large stick in Calandra's left hand began to twirl. She quickly swung it forward, connecting with the head of the man. Not waiting to see how much damage had been inflicted, she pulled Scarlett out of the room and back down the corridor, retracing their steps. There were already other men there with an assortment of weapons, and all keenly looking at Scarlett. Scarlett felt the hand that held her let go, and she heard the whispered words "just stay close".

One of the men stepped forward with a large cudgel in his hand. As he swung it at head height, Calandra ducked, swinging her stick at his ankles, then bending and turning before driving her stick into his chest. Scarlett looked away as she was certain it was penetrating the skin. She wasn't built for this sort of thing. Looking away from more sounds of thuds and cracking skulls, she felt her hand being grabbed again, and she was being dragged back down the stairs.

"We need to be out of here," said Calandra. "Whatever happens, don't leave my side. I can protect you only if you stay close."

As she descended the stairs, Scarlett heard footsteps from behind. Flicking her head, she saw her pursuers, three to four men, all armed, all focusing on her. Then in the melee, something occurred to her. They were man-sized, they looked like men but something was wrong with their faces. The shape of the head, every one of them, was not rounded enough. It was almost as if the face had been squashed in, forcing the top of the head upwards and the chin downwards giving a kind of elliptical quality. She didn't have time to ponder as she heard Calandra take out another one of the men at the foot of the stairs.

"This way," shouted Calandra, dragging Scarlett towards the door. There then came a gunshot. At least, Scarlett thought it was a gunshot. Truth be told, this had only been a guess, for she had never heard a real gunshot in her entire life. It was loud, incredibly loud. Her ears began to ring and part of her felt like feeling over her body in case anything had been hit. But before she could even think about doing it, Calandra grabbed her hand tight, taking her away from the main door and deep into the hotel itself.

"Rodriquez," muttered Calandra to herself, "Rodriguez, where the hell are you?"

Although the hotel itself was not that big, it did seem to be larger on the lower floor, as the corridor cut this way and that, little rooms here and there. Calandra dragged her along the corridor at a rate which Scarlett's mind could not keep up with. A door was opened, Scarlett was flung in followed by Calandra, and the door shut behind them.

"Don't say a word. Keep quiet." And then under her breath Calandra complained once more, "Where the hell is Rodriguez?"

The room they were in appeared to be a store cupboard. Several toilet rolls and other small bottles of chemicals on the shelf, mop at the back of a large collection of hand tiles on the floor. Struggling to know why they were in a dead-end, Scarlett thought that surely the only thing that could happen was that they would be discovered. She looked at the woman who had brought her into the situation. Scarlett saw there was a frosty tinge to Calandra's face and wondered if she was turning to glass. It wasn't that she looked like a statue, but there was a sheen on the skin which was reflecting the light and the images of things around them. Calandra turned and briefly looked at Scarlett, evidently aware of what her eyes were focused on. There was a silent laugh on her lips before she turned back to the door. Scarlett's mind was reeling. Then the strange heads of the men attacking people came back to her mind—a midget and now this lady, this woman whose flesh could reflect images around due to its glassy quality.

Scarlett saw Calandra look inside her jacket and remove a very small transceiver. There were a number of buttons on the device. Scarlett was unaware of what they did, but she watched some sort of code being input on the different buttons by Calandra before the item was replaced. Calandra then motioned for Scarlett to stand back and a hand was placed upon the door they had entered. Scarlett watched a frost form over the door, freezing it into position. The skin on the hands of Calandra turned completely glassy for a moment, and Scarlett could see right through them to the door.

Calandra turned back and saw Scarlett's face. She muttered, "Never seen an Ice Maiden before?" It was just another thing to set Scarlett's mind racing.

Scarlett became aware of something beneath her feet. The room was tiled with large squares of carpet, the sort that are glued on to resist any wear and tear. Scarlett saw Calandra start to smile before pushing Scarlett back into the corner of the small room. Going down on a knee, Calandra started to rip up the tiles on the floor, exposing wooden floorboards underneath. Scarlett could see a hot circle forming on the floorboards before they fell into the dark below Scarlett. She drew a shaky breath, waiting for something else to come up from the dark, but was then surprised by the head of the small man who had driven the van.

"Rodriguez," whispered Calandra, "where the hell have you been?"

Rodriguez didn't answer. He gave a look, shaking his head in the process. He then ducked down back into the black, and Scarlett saw Calandra point that direction. There was nothing to do except follow these people, no chance to stand and have a debate about what would happen. Remembering the faces of the men chasing them, she did not want to meet them again. Scarlett manoeuvred herself into the dark below.

Scarlett squeezed into the hole in the floor and cursed her unknown mother for blessing her with the curves she had. Although not overweight, she had always felt self-conscious about the largeness of her hips, hips she thought she would be better off without. Those hips were now struggling to get through the hole in the floor. She felt Calandra put a hand onto her shoulder and shove down. She anticipated a long drop as Rodriguez's seemed to disappear quickly, but instead the floor arrived almost instantaneously, and she found her own head still stuck above the level of the floorboards.

"Go on your knees," whispered Calandra and drove Scarlett down further. As her eyes entered the dark, Scarlett saw something like a head and assumed it was Rodriguez, and made her way towards it. Her head cracked off some sort of timber beam, and she lowered herself, becoming snugger to the dusty, seemingly concrete floor beneath. She felt someone prodding her back, pushing her bottom further forward. Calandra, seemingly, was not in the mood to hang about.

The situation improved after several minutes, and Scarlett became aware of a larger hole in the distance where light was flooding in. She raced towards it. Unfortunately, she ran into the small man who was her rescuer. She felt Calandra tap on her rear and squeeze past. Gingerly, Calandra approached the light, remaining to one side, and stared out for some time. Then she retreated until she was alongside Scarlett.

"Listen up, little lady, what's about to happen is going to take place very quickly. I'm expecting some backup to arrive in a very fast vehicle to get us out of here. I need you to stay close as I need both hands free. Rodriquez will help, but don't wait for us when you see it. Just run and get on board. Don't look back, don't wait for us, just get on board."

Scarlett could do nothing but nod. At the end of the day, she was stuck with these people until they got to a place and time where the other people were not after her. Scarlett's knees were sore. She had been crawling across what seemed like concrete, that underside of all buildings you never see unless you happen to be unfortunate enough to be setting up the plumbing, or wiring, or other features that were always hidden from view. As they waited in the darkness, her mind reeled back to seeing Calandra's frozen hands, the man in the room with the eyepatch, the elliptical and very, very strange heads.

From their current position, they could hear people moving about, both in the hotel and from the area outside. Scarlett looked ahead to the hole and thought that it led out to the car park of the hotel. The plan must be to get a car, something very close she felt. There would be a time to run hard. Running wasn't her strong point. In that regard she had always hated cross country running. Being somewhat buxom, she always endured stares from the boys when she'd gone on any of the outdoor runs. It wasn't that she was unfit, as she was a strong swimmer and somebody who enjoyed walks, but the body just wasn't built for the jogging motion. Hence, every time she did want to run, she ran alone. But this time she wouldn't be some figure to be laughed at. Still, it was probably better to be laughed at than hunted down.

Scarlett saw Calandra's face light up as the sound of an aircraft could be heard in the distance. Scarlett wondered why she was so excited for how could an aeroplane help? Clearly, it wasn't a helicopter as it didn't make that constant, repetitive sound, indicative of all helicopters. But the arrival of the sound caused Calandra to move to the hole and cautiously peer out. After a few seconds, her hand waved Scarlett and the small man forward. She watched Calandra break her staff down, place it inside her jacket and then remove two handguns. She leaned over to Scarlett.

"We'll step outside to give you cover. Run between me and

Rodriguez. Don't look back, just go straight to the plane."

"Plane? How you going to land the plane here?" whispered Scarlett. "There's no room to land a bloody plane."

Calandra smiled. "Just get on the plane."

Rodriguez exited the hole first. Before Calandra had followed, he was firing off shots.

Scarlett saw Calandra rise to full figure with a single, smooth motion, graceful as a cat. The sound of handguns firing at distant targets caused Scarlett's body to jump, but she managed to force herself to crawl out and was aghast at the sight before. There was a plane sitting at the far end of the car park, but it was not like a plane she'd seen before. Sure, there were tiny wings at the back and the main body, and even the large wings, but the engines she was looking at were facing the wrong way. As far as she knew, most planes, especially the ones with propellers, had the engines in the front. Occasionally, she saw propellers at the rear of the big wings, facing the other direction. But never had she seen propellers that face the sky. How does it fly? Does it go forward?

The questions in her head immediately dissipated as a bullet struck the wall behind her. Focusing her mind, she pushed her body into a run. She fixed her eyes on the aircraft, drove her legs to carry her hips but this time there would be no eyes that gave a damn about how she looked. From the corner of her eye, she saw Calandra firing off rounds with a gun but also starting to receive undue attention from a large number of people getting closer. She had lost sight of Rodriguez, but there was a figure at the aircraft who had emerged from a door in the side.

As she ran closer, the gunfire still raining, she saw that the figure was dressed in a smart suit, pinstripe trousers with black shoes and wearing a bowler hat on his head. He would have been more at home on the stock market or in a 1960's spy movie, but he had one hand clapping his hat to his head and the other reaching for her.

"Wilson," he said, "the name's Wilson, please get inside."

Scarlett gratefully took his hand, which led her inside the aircraft. The interior of the aircraft had a few seats and the piloting area to the front was open with one person sitting at the controls. Scarlett saw Rodriguez enter the aircraft behind her, his smaller frame moving a lot quieter, and she anticipated Calandra's arrival. She found herself being placed in a seat by the Wilson character who then returned to the door and shouted loudly and politely at Calandra. Scarlett felt the aircraft begin to lift somewhat unsteadily. Gunfire was still ringing, and she was sure some were catching the body of the aircraft. From her position, she could also see Calandra in the car park outside. No longer did she have her guns out, but instead had returned to using her long stick and was dispatching several of the strange headed men who had attacked them.

The aircraft was rising. Scarlett was sure that Calandra was going to be left behind as they were well above fifty feet in the air. Wilson had remained at the rear door. Through the window Scarlett could see a rope hanging out of the aircraft. The aircraft began to move forward as well as up and Scarlett saw the engines of the aircraft rotate around the wing, coming more to the horizontal plane, but still not fully level. Looking out the window, she saw Calandra grab the rope and begin to climb. Gunfire peppered her from below. Scarlett looked on in amazement as the woman, whose body had previously gone glassy, now became fully translucent. Shots rang off her.

She was a glass figure inside her clothing. Within a minute, she had climbed the rope and was inside the aircraft.

"Good job," said Wilson, as he headed towards the cockpit. Scarlett watched Calandra take up the seat beside her and marvelled at the clear features the woman displayed. She could actually see right through her face to the other side of the cabin which was a blur. Like looking through a frozen lake or a diamond held up high. Slowly the skin became more opaque before eventually returning to her normal pale white. Now she merely looked like someone from Iceland.

Calandra turned and smiled. "Well, I did tell you I was the Ice Maiden."

4

The Necklace

The only sign of life was her blonde hair as Scarlett submerged everything except her head under the warm water. The rather plush bathroom she was in didn't take away the memories of the past few hours. Everything at the time seemed such a blur, but now that she had a moment to catch up, she was remembering the men and the other things that came after. Also entering her mind was the sight of the people from the coach in various states of damage in the hotel. In this moment of solitude, it was clear that the mind was taking time to adjust, taking time to soak in the situation, just as sure as her body was soaking up the warmth of the water.

After the aircraft left the scene, the windows turned strangely black and Scarlett had no idea where the aircraft had travelled. They couldn't have travelled that far because they landed within twenty minutes of having left. For the whole of the ride, the woman who called herself Calandra had been staring at her, assessing, and Scarlett found it frankly uncomfortable. She felt inadequate beside this ice woman, and not simply because she was quite clearly the inferior when it came to handling large and quite nasty men. The woman was also an antithesis of everything Scarlett was. Where the woman was relatively tall and sleek, she also managed to have a strong and fit profile. Scarlett was plump, short, stubby and somewhat closed, with unkempt blonde hair. This was clearly unfair. Scarlett wasn't overweight—well only a few pounds—and certainly had more curves than the other woman. Whether it was being overweight that produced each curve always played in Scarlett's mind. Still, at least with her body concealed under the surface of the water, there could be no confirmation whether her thoughts were true or not.

How could she think like that at a time like this? People were dead, people were after her, yet some of the first things that came to her was how she looked against this strange but compelling woman. Scarlett brushed away the remaining thoughts, but then realised that the things left afterwards were more horrific. Maybe it was better to do the comparison rather than dwell on the darker matters beyond?

A knock sounded on the door, and she heard a voice tell her that the boss would like to see her as soon as possible. When she didn't reply, the male voice on the other side said that they would be back in approximately five minutes and requested that she be in a state of dress when they arrived. Scarlett initially thought she would stay in the water and let its cleansing properties work its magic on her sore limbs, but when her brain caught hold of the idea that in five minutes time some man was going to walk into this bathroom with her still in the water, she immediately hauled herself out. Standing on a bath mat on the floor, she dried herself down before reaching for some clothing she had discarded beside the bath.

She saw a chair in the corner which held other clothing. There was a simple note on top that said wear these. The thought crossed her mind of keeping her old clothing until Scarlett realised that the clothing was rather drab, functional yes, but still rather drab. It consisted of a large, grey jumper, baggy, certainly not figure hugging, underwear, and some tracksuit bottoms. When she dressed in her clothes and caught a look at herself in the mirror, she realised just how non-descript she looked in the outfit. Again, thoughts of Calandra's tight fitting jeans and black leather jacket and simply how stylish, elegant and, downright sexy she looked, attacked her very bland appearance.

Changing into the clothes provided, Scarlett reassessed herself. The stout boots felt awkward but the blue jeans seemed comfortable enough. The brown t-shirt felt a little tight but she felt her figure just about carried it, and the suede jacket actually was rather swish. However, her hair was a mess. There was a brush on the dresser of the bathroom and Scarlett used it to tackle her long blonde hair before finding a hair tie and finishing off her preening by collecting her hair together in a simple ponytail. Just as she finished, a knock on the door sounded.

"The boss is requesting your presence," said the person on the other side. Realising it was now a woman speaking, Scarlett advised her to come in. It was the woman who had rescued her that entered. Calandra was still in black jeans but the leather jacket had been discarded and the figure hugging T-shirt she was now wearing made Scarlett somewhat jealous. But the woman smiled when she looked at Scarlett.

"Do you feel better for that?" asked Calandra.

"I think *better* is a very strange term in this situation," said

Scarlett. "Never had anything like this happen to me. It seems that my mind keeps focusing on the worse things to think about rather than what I actually saw."

"In my time doing this sort of work," said Calandra, "I find it never goes away. Seeing scenes of people in a state that they should not be in never gets easier, never stops hurting. I'm sorry you had to see that, but unfortunately, it goes with the territory when involved in these sort of things."

"What sort of things are these?"

"That is best left for the boss to explain. He's looking to speak with you."

With that, Calandra took herself out of the room, then stopped momentarily to look around the rather ornate country style bathroom, presumably checking there was nothing else still in the room. Clearly, this was just a chance to slow things down as Scarlett's old clothes were still on the floor yet she made no attempt to either regain them or do anything with them.

Once she had exited the room, she found herself following Calandra like some schoolchild going to the headmaster's office. This lady was silent, but she had a gait that was annoying Scarlett. Someone that trim shouldn't be able to swing her hips like that, looking as though she were on parade, moving about whatever secret headquarters they were in now. Again the absurdity of a comparison, the need to bring down this woman struck. Scarlett realised the defence mechanisms must have been kicking in again.

Scarlett was led along many corridors and up a few stairs on the passage to the boss. Occasionally, a person would go past, sometimes in very smart office wear, and at other times wearing very casual outdoor clothing. Most gave a brief smile, a personable front presented, but she got the idea that behind there was a defence, some sort of wall which said she might get the weather from them but she wouldn't get a lot else. The building seemed to be some sort of country house with many pictures on the walls showing people in very regal poses, but Scarlett didn't recognise any of the faces. Sideboards ran along every corridor, items of crockery placed on them. She had never watched the Antiques Roadshow or any other program about grand items from previous centuries, and Scarlett was unable to identify any of the pieces.

She was much happier when she was at home watching a nature programme of the animals that occupy so much of our world. She seemed to understand the animals more than people. Maybe it was just the way the programmes showed them. When she got the chance, she enjoyed going along to zoos, or indeed any wildlife parks, to stop and stare at the animals. She often spent most of the day there without conversing with any other human, but instead stopped at whatever fence, wall or viewing platform was given and watched the animals work, rest and play. Sometimes they seemed to move closer to her, and she thought they were staring back at her. But perhaps her mind just invented this idea to make up for her lack of human interaction.

They approached a wooden door, and Calandra knocked on it. A simple word to enter could be heard, and Calandra opened the door to a small but very grand looking office. There was a cabinet placed beside the only window. It contained many paintings and other artefacts in small cases. The floor itself was wooden, made up of very stylish boards and looked somewhat worn down and aged. The single window in the office occupied most of one wall and the view beyond was of mountains, green with snow-capped summits. Scarlett drew a breath at the sight before a figure suddenly appeared beside them.

"It's quite a view ma'am, and yes, that's why it's my office."

Scarlett then realised the man before her was the same man that had welcomed her onto the aircraft. He was dressed extremely smartly, still in his trousers and black shoes that he had on before, but now he was in a waistcoat, shirt and tie underneath. She fought for the word to describe him. He reminded her of those businessmen in the city, but unlike their official garb, there was a different strain to this man. As he smiled and extended a hand towards her, she thought of those dancers twirling women around the floor and the ballrooms. Dapper—that was the word—extremely dapper.

"I think I said to you before, but it's probably worth reminding you, the name is Wilson. And very pleased to meet you, Miss O'Meara."

Scarlett got the distinct impression that this man knew a lot already. Even the words *Miss O'Meara* managed to convey that he was being polite, but that he knew everything about her. This was rather unnerving, and she felt her heart rate climbing up, sweat beginning as she thought out a reply. She was walking into a conversation she was very much second-best in. It felt like one of those parties during which she stood at the side and then someone would find her and she wouldn't know what to say. Instead she'd dip her head and withdraw. And hence she found men were just staring at her instead of conversing with her. Was she just not conversing with them?

"Hi. I'm Scarlett. Scarlett O'Meara. But I guess you knew that."

"Indeed, Miss O'Meara, indeed I did, and I know a lot more,

but there's nothing for you to be nervous about. In essence, you have been quite lucky. I realise that you did not ask to be in this situation, yet that doesn't change the fact that you're up to your neck in it. Thankfully for yourself, we were able to get you, to keep you safe from the other parties who were interested in what you had."

"What do I have?" asked Scarlett. "After all this, do I actually have anything? We never found anything. I thought it was still back in the hotel, whatever it is that I supposedly possess."

"I doubt that," said Wilson, "as they were all over the place and, unlike Miss Calandra, I do believe they are equal to searching a building in the same way that we are."

"We? Who is we?" asked Scarlett.

"We, as in the organisation I work for. It is a secret government organisation which monitors threats—bizarre threats from places that most people do not know even exist. We deal with the strange, we deal with that which people don't want to think about, that their minds often struggle to comprehend. We are like the clean-up crew for the terrible, monstrous things that go bump in the night."

Scarlett's face fell somewhat. She realised things were getting a bit odd, but this was a different level. Standing there slightly amazed, she had her hand taken by Wilson who led her gently to a chair in front of his desk. Having deposited her there, he turned, poured a small cup of tea which he then handed to her. Scarlett became aware that Calandra moved into flanking position just off her right shoulder. She looked very different, but she felt like a guard.

"What is it they are after?" asked Scarlett. "Mr. Wilson, do you actually know what they wanted? Because your colleague behind me didn't seem to."

"In fairness to Miss Calandra, at the time we were rather in the dark, but since then we have managed to collect slightly more intel and I believe I know what they were looking for."

Scarlett waited for the man to continue, but he just sat there looking at her "Are you going to tell me?" asked Scarlett.

"Oh," said Wilson, "I thought you just wanted to know if I knew. That's what you asked. I'm kind of programmed to answer only what I'm asked."

"I want you to answer, too," said Calandra.

Wilson at first looked slightly amused, then gave a glance that showed annoyance before breaking into a gentle laugh at the comment. "Please forgive Miss Calandra, as she is getting used to the idea of me running the organisation. My former boss was a good friend of hers, and she worked very closely with him. I'm a somewhat different character. He was very by the book, extremely professional, demanding but didn't have a sense of humour like myself. Sometimes I believe Miss Calandra thinks I'm the light version. She is, of course, entirely wrong in that surmise, and I'm sure time will explain that to her".

Scarlett ignored what politics was going on and instead reiterated the question. "Are you going to tell me what they were looking for?"

"Indeed, dear lady, indeed. It seems that when you had your little skirmish, the one at the service station, it wasn't some sort of sexual assault. I believe the man in question had his hand inside of your clothing for good reason, in that he dropped something, an item of considerable value." Wilson rose to his feet and turned to look out the window. "It's an old item, very old."

"You mean like the things on those antique programmes?"

"Ah, well, Miss, certainly not from those programmes. I doubt anyone on those programmes would realise its true worth. The item in question is a necklace, and at its centre is a small gem, a sort of emerald. But its worth isn't in its monetary value, its worth is in what it enables the bearer to do."

"Are you sure about this one?" asked Calandra. "After all, we had no confirmation, visual or any other means. Are you definitely following these lines, because to my mind, we should be a lot more open and sceptical about what it is and what it's going to be used for?"

"Miss O'Meara, I always value the contributions of my employees, and I always value any input at any time from those around me, but do believe me, I have an understanding here that a lot of others have not reached. And that understanding places you at the centre of all of this."

"Mr. Wilson, could you please tell me what the hell you're going on about? I'm sitting here listening to you prattle on about what is and what isn't, and I'm none the wiser from the time spent with you."

"My apologies, Miss O'Meara, I realise this may be a little strange for a girl from the valleys. By the way that Welsh accent is quite lovely."

"Yes, well, this girl from the valleys is going to get up and walk in a minute," said Scarlett, "because at the moment, as glad as I am that you rescued me from those men, I don't see what this all has to do with me apart from being someone who you believed had something, which I clearly don't."

"Well, they definitely knew you had it. However, I don't think they, or you, understand it. In truth, I don't fully understand this object, I just know a little more than others."

"How am I wearing it? From my underwear to this outfit you seem to have given me, I know everything I've got on at the moment. I've just come from the bath, and I guarantee when I looked around there was nothing on me. As you can tell, I don't even wear jewellery so I think I would notice any new addition."

Wilson sniffed slightly, Scarlett thought rather indignantly, before he walked off to a bookcase in the corner of the room. He drew out a book that had the old stale cover on it, one without pictures whose leather, in which it was clad, was looking the worse for wear.

"You really should look after your books, Mr. Wilson," said Scarlett. "My own back home look a lot better than that."

"Indeed they may, but I doubt you have any books like this. He returned with the large volume, facing Scarlett from the lower side of the table and opened the book to the first page. Scarlett looked and saw some rather old writing and recognised it as English even if it was slightly old English, a form she had never spoken and certainly never spelled like that even with her own dodgy ability with words.

"What's this?" asked Calandra.

"This is one of the oldest books I have in my collection and work that does not come from this world. Don't be fooled by the leather binding around it, which was applied some six to seven hundred years ago in a monastery high in the Alps. This book might be called an encyclopaedia, but that really doesn't justify what it is. This book is quite special. Behold!"

Wilson traced lines in the book three times and then spoke some words that Scarlett struggled to understand. He sounded like he was grunting and it certainly wasn't English. In fact, it didn't sound like a language that came from anywhere near

England or Wales for that matter. Scarlett nearly jumped as the pages of the book began to flip before suddenly stopping open at a page approximately one-third of the way through the book. Scarlett leant forward to see what was there but the pages were blank.

"What was the point of that?" asked Scarlett. "There's nothing there, like some sort of parlour trick."

Wilson smiled, reached forward and tapped the page three more times and there appeared on the page a picture of a rather ornate looking necklace with an emerald at its centre. Beneath the picture was writing. This time the writing was not English; instead, it was a series of hieroglyphs, but not Egyptian hieroglyphs, something similar yet completely different. Scarlett held back a laugh, rather bemused at the whole show.

"Don't worry about the language," said Wilson, "it's a language that even I struggle to read. But we have people who can deal with these things, and they pointed me in the right direction."

"Austerley?" asked Calandra.

Wilson nodded. "Yes, sorry, our walking occultist encyclopaedia, Mr. Austerley, confirmed what was on this page and why we should look for it. It's a very interesting item indeed. Miss O'Meara, may I ask you to stand and come forward to the desk."

Scarlett looked at him, felt a little awkward, but did she was asked. On reaching the desk, she found Wilson leaning over, grabbing her shoulders and pulling forward until she was at a slight tilt.

"Can you remove your jumper for me please?" asked Wilson.

Scarlett looked at him. "I'm expected to just take it off here for all to see."

"I understand the hesitation, Miss O'Meara, trust me there's nothing sexual about what I'm asking. I need you to do this." His eyes were insistent. Scarlett had the feeling that whatever was going to happen was going to happen, so slowly and rather embarrassingly she removed the jumper, dropping it on the floor. She shivered as Wilson reach forward and touched her breast bone murmuring a few words. One moment she was shivering from the touch of a man asking her to do something rather strange, and then the next she was shivering from the sight appearing on her breastbone. Within her skin was forming a green glow and from the green glow emerged a line, a line of gold snaking around her neck. On her skin was the mirror-image of the necklace in the book.

5

The Last Remaining Beastmaster

Scarlett clutched at the necklace. It wasn't separate from her body but rather, was integral with the skin, pronounced but somehow embedded into her person. Both hands ran desperately across her breastbone. How did this get there? Where did it come from and how could she get it off? And what would these people think? All along she had maintained that she knew nothing about concealing anything. She felt her body begin to shudder as a fear and panic ran through. Her vision became unclear as tears ran from her eyes, and she looked up desperately in the direction of Wilson.

"Has she been hiding this all this time?" asked Calandra. Scarlett felt the cold touch of a hand on her shoulder and turned to look into a face that was not showing any mercy.

"I think we should give her our guest room," said Wilson. "I don't believe that Miss O'Meara has been hiding anything but rather that the item itself was hiding, even from her. It is most unusual for it to hide, most unusual indeed, but it will do so in certain circumstances according to my investigator."

"Certain circumstances?" blurted Scarlett. "What the hell

do you mean certain circumstances?"

"Calm down. This will be a shock too, as you are going to learn something about yourself that you never knew," said Wilson. "According to Mr. Austerley, the necklace itself bestows power on anyone to assist with the control of beasts and almost any creature. But to some, and it is a very, very select few, it binds with an ability they already have. For those who can already communicate, those who can already connect with these creatures, it binds itself to them."

"Binds itself? Well, get it off! Just get the thing off me!"

"I'm not sure it'll ever do that," said Wilson. "Indeed, if I were actually able to do that, I'm not sure I would. You see, you're really quite blessed in all this. In fact, this may be a comfort for you, in that you are beginning to see and understand what your role in this life might be."

"Role?" asked Calandra. "What her role might be in life?"

"Yes indeed, role," said Wilson. "Calandra, dear, you are looking at one of the few remaining, in fact probably the only remaining, beast master. However, I do question if that is the correct description. I can't remember if the female takes the masculine or indeed, simply beast mistress. I must look that up."

"Who the hell cares what I take? I don't take! Just what do you mean beast mistress, beast master, beast anything?"

"There are rumours, legends or… in fact, it's a mess, an old mess, tales that are barely written down anywhere. One is a tale of people who could not speak with, converse with animals, but rather changed their minds in a certain form of telepathy. Not the simple creatures, the older ones. Creatures that are, unfortunately, more developed. And usually a lot more deadly."

"Wilson, but you said 'beast mistress'." said Calandra. "I am eight hundred years old, and I have never heard of a beast mistress."

"Individually, it is quite something, quite rare," said Wilson, "but there are many things older than eight hundred years. Many things coming from darker times and darker places.

"Never mind where they come from, never mind what they do. How do you get this off me?" yelled Scarlett.

"In simple terms," said Wilson, "I cannot. I genuinely cannot remove that. I'm not sure many people can. But those who seek it are coming for you, and it won't stop them from killing you. The necklace might remove itself if its host—sorry, that's a rather horrific term—its partner were to die.

"Die? Die? They want to kill me now?"

"No," said Calandra. "Thinking analytically, they would have done that back at the hotel or back in the woods. They think you have something, therefore they are looking to take it back. But they had to know all this, but they didn't understand you were one of them."

"One of them?"

"Yes, one of them, one of whatever it is you are. Whatever it is, and we only have a name, as a description from Wilson, they don't know that you are. Probably quite lucky that way."

"Lucky, how the hell is this lucky?"

"I think our new friend needs a little time," said Wilson and returned to look through the windows at the cold and crisp countryside outside. "I need to obtain something we don't have. Information. Whatever it is that these other parties intend to do with the necklace is still unknown. And they will no doubt try to retrieve the necklace again, so I think we need to make headway ourselves. Rodriguez is capable of getting some more information. In the meantime, I think Miss O'Meara can do with developing her gift."

"Developing? Can I develop it? I don't speak to animals. I don't talk to beasts. I don't do any of this. I think it's made a mistake."

"I imagine it's normal to feel this way, but there has been so few of you in history, I guess normal is probably inaccurate." Wilson smiled. "I'm sure they felt like this, maybe felt worse as they may not have had anyone explain to them what was going on, at least you had that. No, I think that we need to explore your gift but in a conducive environment. It seems to me that trip to the North is required to see an old friend of Calandra's."

"What old friend?" asked Calandra.

"Don't worry, not the boys. I mean the zoo keeper."

"That weasel," said Calandra. "If he tries anything this time, I will break his neck."

Scarlett looked up to see if she was smiling and laughing, in a vain hope that they would be going to someone at least normal, if not nice. But the face was like the body, cold.

"I do not disagree, he is a strange one and certainly in normal society would probably have ended up in a few jail cells with the things he's tried, but there is one thing he's good at. He does run our zoo rather well."

"Your zoo?" asked Scarlett.

"This must all seem rather weird," said Wilson. "I'd rather have more time to brief you before immersing you into our world, but that's not possible. We need to get you moving with using this device effectively. I've the feeling it's going to become rather important. Some time off in the North of Scotland. Calandra with you as your bodyguard and guide."

"I kept her safe from the people back at the hotel, now from the animal pervert," sneered Calandra.

"There is no need for that," said Wilson, "our friend has got enough on her plate. You can take the car," said Wilson," try keeping it low-key. Keep out of the way and keep aware. Now they know that someone else is involved, they may start to use other assets. Make sure you go packing some heat."

"Heat? You trying to be funny?" asked Calandra.

"My wife does say I have my moments," retaliated Wilson, "but this is not one of them."

Scarlett lay back in the leather seat until she felt a normality in the chair's comfort. She went back to a time when she been travelling and trying to sleep as she had been driven the length the country through the night. That journey was comfortable, and there had been no thoughts in her head of creatures, destinies and people trying to come after her. And there had certainly been no drivers beside her that felt like a refrigeration box.

After leaving Wilson, Calandra took Scarlett to get changed into a more appropriate outfit, as she put it. Scarlett wondered if the woman's outfit of black leather jacket over the crop top, black jeans and boots was some sort of the standard issue. No one else in the building seemed to confirm her theory, indeed many were simply wearing suits, making the place look like a remote and detached Whitehall department. Rodriguez met them and Calandra explained that Wilson was wanting him in the main office. He gave a brief smile at Scarlett which was rather bizarre coming from a midget. *That's probably a derogatory term*, thought Scarlett, after all it had been used on her. Pint-sized Welsh fireball was how one boyfriend described her, but then he had been such an idiot. Too many of them were idiots.

Scarlett was kitted out in a set of leather trousers with short ankle boots and a fleece jacket and a T-shirt. The T-shirt they provided was tightfitting which felt quite unusual. Scarlett had usually worn very loose fitting clothes, but Calandra said they just got in the way, especially during a fight. How did that matter? Was Scarlett going to start punching people? She needed to make sure that Calandra realised she wasn't a combatant, but she was being looked after. "Bodyguard," Wilson said, that was straight forward and she would be protected, not part of the fight.

They had gone down to the basement of the building and found a garage. But it was unlike any garage that Scarlett had ever seen. A number of cars, most of them were non-descript but there was one at the end. It looked like a sports car, something any boy racer would drive. *There's something else about it,* Scarlett thought. It was black, the kind of black that shone, but it was more than that. It seemed to stand out for a moment in your mind, then it would be just one of those cars. However, that illusion dispersed the moment you stepped inside.

Scarlett had never known a car with so many buttons and so many screens. Yes, it was a windscreen but on the inside of the windscreen were other things, green lines, numbers and a multitude of indications on the screened area. Calandra said it was a heads up display. Scarlett wasn't sure she could take that much information at once.

However, Calandra seemed pleased that she was getting the car and signed for the keys in a happy fashion.

The women then returned upstairs, finding a kitchen, and Scarlett dined on haggis, neeps and tatties. Passing on the haggis, Calandra explained that she didn't really enjoy ovine stomach.

Soon they were on the move, first along underground roads which was all very strange, especially when they emerged right through some rocks onto a road. They looked like ordinary rocks, and when she turned round and looked back at the road they had entered, it was a normal roadway, but the route they had emerged from was just a rock face. It was dark, for it was the early hours of the morning as the car roared into the Scottish night.

Calandra had obviously driven before. There seemed to be a smile, albeit a small one, across her face as she drove the car around tight corners at speed. Maybe she was just assessing the road ahead as she hadn't used any lights so far. However, the windscreen showed a green glow bringing images to the forefront, something Calandra said was night vision. Scarlett was struggling to comprehend who she was with. It felt like one of those programmes on TV, the spy programmes from an older time of wacky gadgets.

"Best to get some shut eye," said Calandra. "Going to be a long drive."

"You really think I can sleep? You have to understand this is my first secret organization and 'my first curse.'"

"Curse?" asked Calandra. "What curse?"

Scarlett instantly became indignant. "What curse? This necklace that has joined onto me. It's unusual for devices to take a hold of people, to become part of the skin, get under the skin. I realise it might be normal to you, but this is anything but normal to me. I just really want rid of it."

"It's hardly a curse," said Calandra. "You got something that can lift your powers, something to make it something better, just an extension of yourself. Bit like my staff, and the other weapons are just an extension of myself."

"You're just used to weird." Scarlett saw Calandra raise her eyebrows. "Your skin changes. It beggars belief what happens to it. You turned to ice," said Scarlett. "I saw it change, your body went clear."

"Translucent is the word," said Calandra, "not clear. Clear doesn't give the full impression, so to speak."

"I think you've made my case. That's not normal. He also said you're eight hundred years old. So like I said, you do weird, I don't."

"And you think that makes me immune to it? You think I don't struggle? I just take this all in my stride as another normal day at the office? You have no idea."

"You can turn to ice, you can become something else. It must make it a lot easier, it must make it…"

"Easier?" said Calandra. "Easier…, you have no idea. You have no idea what this cost me."

They travelled in silence, but Scarlett kept casting a glance at the driver who was now fully focused on the road ahead. There was no indication of pain, except in the corner of her eye, in the vicinity—a tear. It seemed to be a tear, but it was held there. Looking at the amount of water within the tear, it should have spilled over but instead it seemed suspended at the duct. And then it wasn't, as she blinked and there was the most imperceptible crunch and a little piece of ice fell to the floor.

"Who was he?"

"Who was who?"

Scarlett pressed. "Who was he?"

"It doesn't matter and I don't want to talk about it. Suffice it to say the price was costly, and that it cost me someone else. I don't talk about it."

Scarlett took the hint. Calandra wasn't the warmest person to talk to, and she wasn't going to be forthcoming. Scarlett tried to turn her head and bury it into the seat.

After a short while, they emerged onto the motorway. Scarlett realised the lights on the car were switched on. Calandra was also holding to the speed limit, something which she had previously not done when they had been driving along in the dark. The motorway was all but deserted, the occasional headlight coming the other way on the other side. Scarlett glanced at her watch, but it wasn't there.

"Missing a clock?" said Calandra.

She is always watching, thought Scarlett. *Guess that's a bodyguard's job, keep an eye on what I'm doing.*

But it was a little disconcerting. Scarlett wondered if she could read faces as well. There was an awkwardness being with someone that you did not trust and did not know. She wished there was a way out of this nightmare, some way to just pack it up and head back. She felt torn, torn between heading back to the drab life that she had been cursing not that long ago, and embracing this parade of the strange.

We're off to the zoo, she thought.

She'd never heard of one at the far north of Scotland, right at the top. But then again, it was unlikely to be a public one as everything else so far had been in the shadows. What do you keep in the shadows? It seemed to speak of higher creatures not your normal animals. It made Scarlett wonder and dream, fanciful dreams that brought forth creatures from myths and legends. When she was growing up, she had read most of the Norse, Greek, Roman and Celtic myths. She was familiar with a number of rather strange creatures, familiar in the sense of the book, not first-hand. But that's all they were: myths and legends. She'd probably get to see a tiger, elephant and other such animals at the zoo.

The car lights on the road went out, and the windscreen changed onto night vision. The engine roared as the car suddenly sped up, and Scarlett was forced back into her seat. She turned and saw Calandra, an image of concentration. She scanned other dials and screens within the car. There seemed to be nothing, no indication that something was wrong, but quite clearly Calandra was worried. Her face was grim as she gripped the wheel holding onto the car, and Scarlett thought it must be doing at least a hundred if not a hundred and twenty mph. And then she heard it. There was a whooshing sound, something akin to a train passing by and a faint shadow as something passed over the top of the car. It was definitely a shadow, but the night vision make it awkward to understand quite how big it was or what it was, for that matter, but it came back and that train sound passed over again.

"Just hold on tight," said Calandra, teeth gritted.

Scarlett nodded. She was amazed at the speeds they were travelling at but something kept sweeping past them. The car was struck on the roof, and Scarlett felt it rear up onto two wheels then onto one side before it clattered back onto the road and raced again. Calandra seemed to be a step ahead and reached behind for something. But then, unbelievably, there appeared giant claws in the road ahead. They were racing towards the car and each was as big as a car. Large talons ripped into the roof above Scarlett's head, and she felt the car being flung into the air, like an out-of-control fairground ride during the spin. Scarlett heard an almighty crash and felt glass breaking in from the car windows. The car continued to spin. She felt cold and received a sprinkling of glass as the window shattered.

The car stopped spinning, and Scarlett felt herself being dragged out of the window. Unbelievably, Calandra was there and pulled her to the back of the car. Scarlett was holding one of Calandra's hands and in the other the staff she had seen before was growing to its full height. This gave reassurance to Scarlett, but it was quickly smashed as an almighty roar went over the top of the car. Scarlett watched Calandra glance up above the car and her face changed to one of horror. But Scarlett froze, part of her did not want to move. The necklace on the breastbone seemed to be taking on a life of its own, and she could feel a second heartbeat. Curiosity took over Scarlett who glanced above the roof of the car to see what had made the almighty noise.

She saw talons as big as herself. She saw the legs, strong and leathery, and she felt the beat of the wings. Then she saw the head with the teeth, the green eyes, and she thought to herself, *That's a dragon!*

6

A Shadowy Encounter

The enormous creature pulled the car out of the way, exposing both women from their shelter. Calandra stood up, her staff spinning crazily and stepped in front of Scarlett. The dragon reached for her, but received a number of hits from the speedy staff. Ignoring the strikes, it caught Calandra's side, sending her crashing across the motorway. It then moved forward with its mighty talons scraping on the asphalt, its eyes intent upon Scarlett. She screamed and turned away, suddenly engulfed by the dragon's claw. Feeling it leap into the air, she panicked but it carried her in its claw, the pressure on her enough to hold her, but not to do any damage. She continued screaming, sudden shock erupting through her voice so that the scream came out broken. From far below she heard Calandra shouting in an attempt to call back the dragon, to take its attention back onto her, but the beating of wings showed this course of action to be wholly fruitless.

I have you now. The voice came into her head and she started. There were words there but her ears hadn't picked anything up. Instead, the voice was just there. It was an American voice, a voice that said I'm in charge, a voice that said you're mine. Scarlett had her hand pinned to her breastbone because she felt a pumping, like something was alive. In the dark of the dragon's claw, she found the whole area being lit up by a greenish glow. Looking inside the top of her T-shirt, she saw that the necklace, the one grafted into the skin by some means unknown, was luminous green and ornate.

Without thinking, she began to talk back to the dragon. Whereas the dragon had spoken in her mind, she spoke out loud. "Why have you got me? Who is it that sent you? Why am I here?"

They want you. The Masters have sent me, the one to give me gold, the ones I will betray eventually.

Scarlett stood inside the claw, her brain struggling to take in all that was happening. It wasn't that long ago that she didn't even think these animals could exist. Now here she was, who knows how many feet in the air, trapped inside the claw of one. The beating of the wings continued and who knew how far away she was now from her so-called protector. Calandra's voice was no longer audible, she was on her own.

"Put me down!" She wasn't quite sure why she had said it, but she said it as if she would be obeyed. There was a sudden turning of wings, a sudden drop in altitude which almost made her sick, before she was gently set down on the ground. She picked herself up from the ground and stood before the mighty dragon which had so recently been hell-bent on carrying her away.

She cast her eyes around in the moonlight, wondering what to do next. She was in a field on the side of a hill, surrounded by trees and for that she was glad. Who knew how many people could come running if she had been in plain sight? Then again, it was dark, another godsend. What to do? She looked up at the dragon that seemed to be almost in a trance. Its eyes seem to show it was in conflict, struggling within. Scarlett was unsure of what she was hearing, the sense of balance within the dragon, fighting to do something it couldn't. And then she thought about what Wilson had said. 'Beast mistress.' Beast master sounded better, but she was a woman and so maybe it was mistress she should use. No, maybe Madam? No, that had particular connotations. Master? The dragon talked about the other master who had given gold, yet Scarlett was giving nothing and it behaved like a pet dog.

"Flap your wings." There was a gentle whishing and look again in the dragon's eye showed that it was doing something it was fighting not to do. "Open your right claw." The claw was opened. *This is almost too easy,* thought Scarlett, *way too easy.* "Take me back, take me back to the car."

The dragon looked at her almost quizzically. "You know what I mean?" asked Scarlett. "Take me back to where you found me," she said. Almost instantly Scarlett was picked up gently but again enclosed. There was a sudden and quick increase in altitude with wings beating hard. Scarlett realised she was being transported back. It was only a few minutes before she landed gently down on the motorway where all was now quiet. There was no sign of traffic. There was no sound of anything. There was no Calandra.

Scarlett reckoned that Calandra might be hurting from the dragon after that rather solid thump she'd been given. She certainly wasn't evident on the motorway. The car lay battered and with its windows smashed, but for the amount of force it had been thrown with, it looked remarkably intact. Again, the idea that Calandra may be hiding because of the dragon came to Scarlett, and she decided to send the beast away.

"Listen to me," Scarlett said to the beast. "Take yourself off from here, take yourself as far away from me as possible. I do not want to see you ever again. Do you understand me?"

Yes, Mistress, said the voice in her head. Without hesitation, the dragon leapt to the air with wings beating. The wind generated flowed over Scarlett, sending her blond hair into a frizzy. She reached up and tried to brush it aside with her fingers but then wondered why she was worried about such looks at this time of the morning. Looking around, she couldn't see Calandra and decided to search the roadside. The glass from the window of the car crunched under her feet but she saw nothing. She returned to the car and now realised there was something missing from outside. There was a large gap in the underside of the car as well as if something had forced its way out, but she was confused as to what.

On the far side of the road, something had moved. There wasn't much moonlight but it was enough to reveal a moving shadow. Scarlett didn't wait. She turned and ran off the motorway then up a large slope into a heavily wooded area. Behind her came the confirmation that she had been right. There was a shout and then repeated shouts back, instructions to find her.

Scarlett ran as hard as hell ahead of them and despite the blood pumping through her head and her ears, she could hear the commotion behind her. They were being subtle like some tracker on the Savannah instead of racing after the cheetah having seen its prey. She needed to get out of here quick, find somewhere to hide. Once she was running, Scarlett was aware that there was something on the edge of perception that she couldn't quite make out. It was a voice. No, wait, not a voice, a consciousness, something she could feel inside. And it was in a state of flight, in a state of panic at the signs around it. *Just like me*, thought Scarlett. Just then she caught a glimpse of a large stag running ahead of her. Desperately thinking, she said, "Stop!" to the air. The stag waited, turning its neck to look straight at her.

Scarlett was caught up in wonder as the mind of the stag flowed into hers. She always wondered what it was like to be free. *Flight, flight, too many noises, too many sayings. Have to run, have to get away.*

"Run with me?" asked Scarlett. The stag waited for Scarlett to catch up with her and then matched her speed. This caused the stag to go into a trot as Scarlett was not keeping up with her animal Sherpa.

They are not far from us. They are close.

Yes, thought Scarlett, *they are close. I need to hide, I need refuge.*

"Show me refuge," said Scarlett. She put her hand on the back of the neck of the beast, taking hold of its hair in her hand. It turned sharply up an incline, making it difficult for Scarlett to keep running with it. Despite the slow pace for the creature, this was somewhat more than Scarlett was used to. Not taking that gym class at the turn of the year was starting to annoy her.

The creature turned sharply several times into an even more heavily wooded area. Scarlett suddenly realised she had been taken inside a ruined building. The building itself was only built on three sides. In its heyday, it may have had several stories but at this point in history only the ground and the first floor were evident. The first floor had only a small area remaining. The area in question was higher than Scarlett and also seemingly out of reach. There were some old steps, but they had fallen away at some point meaning there was a large gap between them and the little space of floor above. Scarlett knew she could never make that jump on her own. In her mind, she saw a solution—a solution she never imagined she could make happen. But the voices were behind, were shouting louder now, and she had no option but to believe in herself.

"Hold still." The stag held its tracks and Scarlett flung her arms around his neck and threw herself onto its back. She could hear the mind saying to get off, something in there was fighting against this wholly unnatural action. "Up the stairs onto that floor," she said. The beast never hesitated despite the obvious conflict running in its mind. But its agility surprised Scarlett, the stag leapt from the steps and made the jump without hesitation. Having landed on the first floor, the creature stopped and Scarlett slipped off into the shadows behind it. *Now just stand there. Hide me. It's me they want, not you.*

The great beast was silhouetted in the pale moonlight shining through the clouds. Scarlett hoped that this would send them off the track as she curled herself into a small ball up against the apex of the two walls that the first floor was connected to. It was dark, it was damp. Above all, it was out of sight. In her mind she could hear the beast screaming that they needed to get away. It was speaking of all the signs which were coming towards it, but the overriding call of its senses was for it to flee. But she told it in her mind to stay put. The voices were so close she didn't speak lest she give away her position.

The sounds of the people coming after them grew closer,

much closer. She believed she could hear some people below searching around the ruins. There was a shade and somebody calling up for her. Scarlett was desperate to know where they were, desperate to know how she could flee from this situation if she had to. She felt herself saying to the beast *what do you see? Where are they? Show me what you know?* These words were almost involuntary, coming from somewhere else inside. And then to her surprise, she shut her eyes. She could see men scrabbling around the bottom of the structure she was in, another looking around searching every nook and cranny. And then one looked directly at her.

"What's out there?"

She saw the man who was pointing at her, clad in black with a gun by his side. Scarlett was unsure what sort of gun, but it certainly looked capable of firing off many rounds at a time. He also had some sort of goggles on, they looked to her like a ski mask. He was dressed in black and should have been well camouflaged in the dark but she seemed to be seeing with a greater clarity than usual. Despite the fact he was now pointing his gun straight at her, she didn't have any fear of being seen. For a moment, she tried to rationalise this but then she realised she was looking through the eyes of the stag.

"It's only a stag."

"The area's all clear, only creatures hiding here. And moonlight."

The second voice had authority, and Scarlett kept to the shadows whilst she listened to the men disappear. In her mind, she intimated to the stag to look around, and it trotted to the edge of the building. She waited a good ten minutes and then checked the entire building surrounds by sending the stag down. *There's nothing there, they have moved on.*

As the stag moved further out, Scarlett felt the connection between them waning and the strength of mind of the creature returning. As this bond grew weaker, the stag suddenly turned, kicked and ran off into the night. Scarlett lay back against the wall breathing heavily. Where did she go from here? Who knew where in Scotland she was? But she knew she needed to move soon in case the men decided to double back.

Despite the adrenaline flowing from the fear inside, Scarlett's mind set upon practical matters. How was she to get down from the ledge? Picking herself up, she wandered to the edge and looked down. The drop was not that large. *Not quite twice my height,* she thought, but that's what comes from being a stumpy arse. She was sure that Calandra probably would have somersaulted off the ledge and landed on her feet. *But we small and compact people,* she thought, *will have to do this with a little bit less refinement.*

Getting down on her hands and knees, she reversed herself to the edge and let her feet start to dangle off as she hung on tight. She had hoped the motion would be gentle and she could hang there, letting go to drop the last couple of feet to the floor. Instead, once she had dropped her feet over, she slid back rapidly, failed to grasp the edge with her hands, and then landed on her backside and the damp grass below. Feeling the pain in her coccyx, she took a moment sitting there in the grass. It was then she became aware of something, something close. She flicked her head around looking for any of the men that might have come back, but she could see none. She tried to reach out with her mind for an animal that was close by. There were some, but she was sure that they were not the presence she was feeling.

The far wall of the building was in shadow, but she could see variations in that shadow. It was as if something was rippling along the wall. Something was there, in the dark watching her. She tried not to panic, but her heart was beating fast. She could feel her throat going dry. Something was there.

She jumped to her feet, turned and ran for the exit. Something grabbed her leg and she tumbled back to the ground, falling face down then rolling over to where she was on her back facing the sky. She felt a presence on top of her. It moved quickly and she felt herself pinned to the ground.

"You are hers?" The voice was low, threatening. Scarlett tried to get out but the shoulders were pinned. Unsure where this voice was coming from, she tried to look around but found her vision was blurred. The surroundings were there, and she could see them but it was like looking through a bathroom window, right in front of you.

Scarlett felt something brush her face. It was like a hand but felt colder. She had been touched by Calandra's hands, and the chill from them was different. The sensation from it wasn't like that of ice cream on your skin but instead carried a sense of dread. She tensed as the cold hand brushed across the cheek and then ran down the nape of her neck. She felt her t-shirt being moved down exposing a breastbone. The necklace and her skin glowed, a green light that should have lit up the area around but instead exposed the shadow. She stared at the area above her. She was sure there were outlines of a face. A hand ran across a breastbone and back round the other side of her neck, cradling her cheek for a moment. "Yes," said the voice, "you are hers."

Scarlett had had enough of this thing and desperately tried to twist and roll away from a situation. But when she moved, she felt pressure being applied against her. It was like a man was holding her down. She went to raise her arm but found her wrist forced back to the ground and then the other one. There was pressure down at her ankles forcing them to the ground. She felt at the mercy of him, whatever he was.

"She was feisty too. You get that from your mother, one of the Welsh assembly, you're all wild women, you Welsh. But you are a rather fine breed."

The voice changed to heavy breath. It was like she was being examined, looked at. While she was still fully dressed, she felt exposed as a hand ran down her face, round to the back of her neck, caressing but it didn't feel enjoyable. But it was the caress of something dominant, something seeking to control. And what was annoying Scarlett at the moment, was that it *was* fully in control.

"He didn't need to hire them. He didn't need to…I would always find you. Those men don't know what they're doing, little guns and their search patterns. The dragon was a good idea to find you, but how he didn't know what you would do surprised me. From the moment I saw you, I knew you were hers. The shape…you have a shape and you have a passion. It's been hidden for so long, but now I see it. Taking the dragon, forcing it to your will as if it didn't have a will at all. He's underestimated you, but don't worry, my dear, I haven't."

She felt a hand and then a cheek, then something touched…. Maybe it was a kiss? But whatever it was, it was unwanted. This seemed like a violation. And she wanted desperately to be free of it. With every ounce of strength, she tried to kick, she tried to shake and eventually she screamed

"Scream what you want, it's just you and me. It was just your mother and me at one point. She fought me but I was too strong for her… I was too strong for her. And I'm too strong for you. Don't make a mistake, submit. I wouldn't want to kill you as well."

"I never knew my mother," blurted out Scarlett. "I didn't even know my father. And they don't know you. Let me go," she said quietly and then at the top of her voice yelled, "Let me go!"

"Never," said the dark voice. "Never."

Scarlett felt helpless. The hand hovered over her face again, then slid down to the nape of her neck. She felt another hand touch her side and tears began to emerge. If only she could get help. If only…

There was a shape beyond the shadow, something beyond this man, this creature that was above. Through the shadow, Scarlett saw a hand reach into the darkness above. And the shadow became clearer as it began to turn cold. Crystals of ice ran across the image, and Scarlett knew he was a man as an outline was traced in ice. A long pointed nose and cruel lips became evident as well as sharp eyes above. Just as the full figure became apparent struggling over her, he was picked up by two hands and thrown into the far wall. The shadow disappeared, leaving a warrior looking down at her. A leather jacket, the dark top underneath and the slender but powerful legs that led into the black boots. Her protector had returned.

"Move!" said Calandra.

7

Safe House

Scarlett grabbed the cold hand and let Calandra lead her out of the ruins. She wasn't sure where she was going, and at the speed that Calandra was leading her, she wasn't about to stop her to find out. They darted this way and that, seemingly never in the same direction, always roundabout routes, always ducking under branches here and there.

Calandra never once looked back. All the time she just kept hold of Scarlett's hand and kept charging ahead. Time and again her feet were slipping, and Scarlett was struggling to keep up. She realised as an athlete, she was Calandra's inferior, and once again thoughts of how she looked, how she moved, paled in comparison to Calandra. In times of greatest anxiety, it seemed her default mode was to ponder her body rather than the situation. Maybe this was because she could do something about her own body, although she never had. Maybe it was because looking at the danger was much worse.

Scarlett could hear people moving about in the undergrowth but Calandra never hesitated, moving swiftly to new places with what seemed like a cursory glance in that direction. *How does she do it? She must be more adept at this than she lets on because so far we haven't encountered anyone.* It was after twenty minutes of running that they broke the cover of the trees and emerged at a bank leading up to the road.

"Stay here," said Calandra. "Don't move, hardly breathe, whatever you do, don't make a noise."

Scarlett nodded. She was feeling reasonably comfortable that they were escaping well and were clear of any people, but this morning had cut her to the core. Though they must still be close. She saw Calandra run further down the bank and then begin to grab an object hidden in the trees. After a few moments working at the object, Calandra wheeled out a small motorbike. It seemed more the scrambler type suiting cross-country rather than a road bike, and Scarlett got a dizzy feeling that she was gonna have to join Calandra on it.

After a false start, the engine kicked into life. Calandra headed straight for Scarlett, spinning the bike around and shouting "get on" over the noise of the engine. Despite anxieties about what was to happen and whether or not she was going to be any use as a passenger, Scarlett jumped onto the back of the bike and wrapped her arms around Calandra's waist. During their journey exiting from the ruins, she had managed to lose her hair tie and her long blonde hair was falling out behind. Calandra's was still sitting in its ponytail, which was fortunate, as if her hair had been cascading then Scarlett would not have been able to see anything.

The bike roared again and Calandra took them straight up the bank onto the road. As they left all the madness of the last hour behind, they raced along, presumably as fast as the motorbike could go. Scarlett put her head down into the back of Calandra's shoulders. The night was cold and crisp and the wind had been flowing into her eyes. She was unsure how Calandra was able to keep going. Surely she should be getting dust in her eyes at this speed, but the women never seem to flap at all. Mile after mile they carried on into the night and Calandra never changed. The hills were becoming larger, but the road was still small, well clear of main routes. And now the snow began as they presumably moved higher up in altitude. From the few times she looked up, Scarlett noticed they were moving onto smaller roads, more off the beaten track. The roads were not clear from snow but were becoming covered. As they sped on, they encountered continued snowfall and a blizzard began driving hard into the two women. Scarlett began to shiver, notably so, causing Calandra to turn round and look at her companion. Then without warning the bike left the road and headed towards a small farmhouse.

Parking the bike beside the house, Calandra told Scarlett to wait and then disappeared around the other side. Looking around, Scarlett saw that she was in a small expanse beside the house. Presumably, underneath the snow was flat as it was not broken up by any plant life. In her mind, she could see this being the parking space of the house and decided it was level, unlike most of the rest of the area. There was water in motion nearby which could be seen in the moonlight, and the snow lay right up to the edges of this flowing river. The grassy tufts barely sticking through the snow might have indicated where the bank was, but there was a serenity, calm in this moment. But then again, she was bloody freezing.

Calandra emerged from behind the building and waved at Scarlett to join her. She scurried off the bike and followed to find the door was open at the side of the house. Inside, she saw Calandra building a fire at a small grate on the far wall.

"Close the door behind you," said Calandra. "I'll try and get some heat going."

"Where are we?" asked Scarlett.

"We're in a special place," said Calandra. "A safe house. Not sure just how safe it's going to be in the long run. We'll stay here, but not for long. Need to warm you up again. Got the impression you were beginning to freeze on the back of the bike."

"Freeze…I was more than frozen. Don't you feel the cold?"

"Is that some sort of joke? I don't feel the cold. Some people say I am the cold."

Scarlett couldn't think of doing anything else but nodding. Calandra didn't seem in a mood to explain the quip. She looked around to see if there was anything else in the cupboards that adorned the wall. It took an exhaustive search before a really old tin of chicken soup was found at the rear. As was her habit, she checked the date and realised it was well past its time. She put it back down.

"What's wrong?" asked Calandra. "It's in a tin, it's fine. Open it, stick it on a gas burner and get warm."

Scarlett was flagging, but after a small search she found a tin opener. Opening the can, she wondered where the saucepan would be. Another search revealed it beneath the sink, and she happily threw the soup into the pan and began to heat it on the gas burner.

"Now that the fire has started," said Calandra. "Get your frozen rear in front of that."

They exchanged places and shortly afterwards, Calandra brought over a hot mug of a somewhat out of date chicken soup.

"Totally fine," said Calandra, testily.

Scarlett took a sip of the liquid and almost choked from the heat. Despite this, it tasted good and she clinched the mug. Remembering her manners, she offered it to Calandra. Calandra seemed rather reticent but took a sip and then handed it over to Scarlett. When Scarlett looked to return it again, she was told that she needed it more and to just get on with it and drink. Something was bothering Calandra. Before she watched Scarlett like a hawk, reading a face during every comment but now she was distracted.

"Okay then, what is it? Tell me what's up because you're acting funny."

Calandra turned her head and looked straight at Scarlett. Once again she seemed to be sizing up, judging whether this was the right moment for whatever comment she was about to make.

"Who are you? I mean, who really are you?" remarked Calandra. "You tell us your name's Scarlett O'Meara and you act as if you don't know what you're doing, acting as if you are some sort of novice in all this, a first timer in this world of craziness and nonsense. But then you subdue a dragon, and a dragon that was happily tossing a car to pieces. And then there's that thing…man…whatever… back in the ruins. Knew you by name, it knew your mother, it knew plenty about you, almost intimate, and the way it dealt with you. It wasn't some creature just after something, trying to take something back off of you. There was a malevolence in there, but it was personal. It wanted something from you but more than that, first and foremost it wanted to humiliate, dominate or something like that. It had a past with you, this was no fresh experience for it. In some shape or form it knew you. I don't. So before we go any further, you're going to sit on your backside and tell me exactly who you are."

Scarlett's face dropped at this turn of events. She tilted her head, letting the blonde hair fall down and shield her face from Calandra's.

"Your guess is as good as mine; I don't know what he wanted. But I do know he thought it was personal. And if he knew my mother, understand this, I didn't. I was an orphan, I was abandoned. I never knew my mother, and I never knew my father. The only people I ever knew were the only good people who raised me, my foster parents. And you can check with your Mr. Wilson about that, but that's all I know about where I come from. I was raised in the valleys, spent most of my life in the valleys but now I...I just don't know. You tell me what this is, you solve this because it's got nothing to do with me."

"You can play that tune if you want, but you tell me how you sent a dragon packing. I was full on for that, I would have had to take it out. I'm not sure I could have... But you sent it away without hesitation. You were able to make it disappear. Tell me how?"

"I don't know," said Scarlett. "I hear them, I hear animals. I didn't used to, even with the necklace that was put on, not until whatever Wilson did to it happened. But I could hear the dragon, I could talk to the dragon and evidently, I could command the dragon. But I also looked through the eyes of other animals when we took flight. I don't know why; I just know it does. I just don't know why."

Calandra, seemingly unsatisfied, grabbed the poker and annoyed the fire. Then she stood up and walked around the room before laying her jacket on the floor. She knelt down and folded it up before turning and lying on her back, using the jacket as a pillow. Scarlett sat huddled by the fire, unsure if the cold she felt was from the room or from her protector. Once again, she began comparing the two of them. *How dare she take that attitude, I'm the one here who doesn't know what's going on. It's their world they got me into, not something I did. How can she be so cold?*

She would be cold. She was cold after all, practically ice. *Why should you expect anything from this person?* Scarlett watched Calandra lying there, swearing she was asleep as her chest rose up and down in slow rhythmic time. *Just because she comes to my rescue, doesn't mean she can keep badgering me with these questions! Maybe I should get out of here,* thought Scarlett. *Maybe I should just go hide, get a bus to somewhere else, and get off the radar. I could talk to some animals and keep out of the way. After all, they traced the car, not me. It wouldn't know where I am, wouldn't know where to start. Yes,* she thought, *time to go.*

Scarlett stood up as quietly as she could and tiptoed to the door. She opened it as gently as possible and was delighted when it made no sound. However, the chill of the nocturnal air took her breath away, but she continued out into the night. Closing the door behind her, Scarlett started across the snow-covered grass ahead. She was walking for approximately a minute before a familiar figure appeared in front of her. Calandra was standing in just a T-shirt and black jeans, boots half covered by snow.

"You sound like an elephant leaving places," said Calandra. "It's also pretty damned heavy, this snow, if you really are as much of a novice in all this as you claim to be. You might not be experienced, but we are and I can guarantee you will like the others searching for you a lot less than us. They sent a dragon for you. They came with a shadow man and goons with guns. The fact is, all I've ever done is protect you".

The wind bit into Scarlett, the snow driving against her face, and she resented how this woman could stand there, obviously inadequately dressed, and yet without flinching.

More annoyingly, there was nothing she could do. *I can leave, but Calandra will track me down in no time. Everywhere I go, she would be there. There's also the fact I have no idea where I am going or how to get there.* Maybe it was the Welsh in her, or short person syndrome, or maybe she was just hacked off, but this idea had been dumb and she was defeated.

Scarlett turned around and walked back to the house. She assumed Calandra was following her but she heard no footsteps. *That's the trouble with these secret agent types, you couldn't keep tabs on them.*

On entering the house, she retook a position beside the fire, warming herself again. Calandra came in and knelt down beside her at the fire. Scarlett watched her eyes cast over, and then Scarlett dipped her head almost in shyness.

"What is it with you?" asked Calandra. "Marching out headstrong like that and then come back in here. You backed down, almost shy. Bet the men love that wildness followed by the contrition."

"What do you know about it?" asked Scarlett. "As if you have any trouble with men."

"Trust me, you wouldn't believe the trouble I have."

The women looked at each other for a moment. Scarlett wondered what the comment meant. But there was no way she was going to get an advantage like that, sit and listen to her sob story. Calandra said she was a protector, well then, she could damn well protect her. For such a big organization, Scarlett was wondering where they all were. Now that trouble had happened, she thought Calandra would have some way of accessing, calling up Wilson, getting more people to them.

"Wondering why it's just us?" asked Calandra. "That's my decision, no one else."

Scarlett peered at her, wondering what was behind this, wondering if there was some sort of personal agenda going on. "Why then?" asked Scarlett. "Explain yourself."

"Explain myself? Don't be tetchy. They were able to follow us and that bothers me. We left in a car that went dark and can be seen only when we got onto the motorway. And then again, maybe they know how to find us. Could be that necklace, but if it is, then you're really in trouble. Could be something else, could be somebody back at headquarters. Whenever it is, I'm undertaking measures to make sure it won't happen again. I can't do anything about the necklace, not even rip it off your neck. I don't know what that will do, and I'll still need to carry it. But I can keep clear of head office."

Calandra got up and walked towards the windows. There was only the firelight and Calandra was careful not to expose any light to the outside world as she looked through the window.

"There's no one here at the moment, so you can sleep. I'll stay awake then worry about getting on the move before anything happens but hopefully we're good for now, you get a little bit of rest because we still have some distance to go."

"We're still going to the zoo?" asked Scarlett.

"Yes, but you may not like how we get there."

***

Scarlett opened her eyes to find a light filling the house.

Calandra had opened only one curtain apparently, but the light was so bright it seemed to illuminate the whole room. Calandra was pulling on her jacket and zipping up.

"Time to get going," said Calandra. "It's nearly midday. We probably should move at night but we can't stay here much longer. If they can trace you through the necklace, we need to keep on the move."

"One minute then." Scarlett groggily got to her feet. Her head ached, and she felt the cold numbness in her bones. Scanning around hoping that there was some other form of food that she could eat when she suddenly remembered that last night there was only the chicken soup. *Oh well,* she thought, *time to get going.*

The women got back onto the motorcycle and Calandra opened up the throttle and they set off along the small road they had previously come along. The sky was blue, the sun was up but a layer of pure white snow was all they could see covering whatever blemishes were hidden beneath. Once again, Scarlett dipped her head behind Calandra's shoulder. She was almost still asleep but the bumps of the motorcycle kept her awake. It wasn't clear how much sleep she had managed the previous night, but with all of the excitement, she certainly was in need of more.

They continued uneventfully for what seemed to be approximately four hours. They passed mountains and the terrain became gradually flat. Light was beginning to fade again, and during one of the short breaks they took, Calandra seemed happy. The breaks were not for comfort, however. Whenever Calandra had seen a car parked by the roadside with no one about, she carefully refilled the tank of the motorcycle by siphoning off from the car. *She really isn't going near anything where we can be spotted*, thought Scarlett.

When the sky turned dark, Scarlett could see that the sea was ahead. *We must have driven the full length of Scotland.* They started off road, across country, but Scarlett could see that it was only a half-mile or so to the shore. Once they were well clear of the road, Calandra indicated that Scarlett should get off. When she was clear, Calandra dropped the bike and covered it by breaking off some branches from a nearby tree. The cover was very rudimentary, but then the snow that was thrown on top did seem to be a sufficient camouflage.

Having satisfied herself that the bike was covered, Calandra crept up beside Scarlett. Slightly crouched, Calandra was always looking around, always scanning the terrain. Scarlett kept in line behind her, one of Calandra's hands dragging her forward. Scarlett wished she had just gone on alone without her, because as always the cold of Calandra's touch sent a shiver down her.

"Over there," whispered Calandra.

Scarlett looked where Calandra was pointing, but struggled to see anything. Calandra pointed out several other places, but again, Scarlett was at a loss to know what she was looking at. It was now clear and bright with a full moon shining down, but even so, Scarlett couldn't make anything out. They circumvented around the areas Calandra pointed to, gradually making their way towards the sea. At one point to cross a road, Calandra ran at full pelt dragging Scarlett roughly and then secreted them in the snow, looking for anyone following. A short time after that, they reached a cliff edge down to the sea.

Scarlett saw waves crashing beneath, the wild spray tumbling through the air before the water crashed back to the rocks. She was somewhat confused as to why they were standing on the edge of a cliff when if anyone came at them there was nowhere to go. *Also where was this zoo? You can hardly keep it here on the edge of a cliff side. It might have been a great view, but in practical terms it was an animal enclosure nightmare.*

"I'm afraid we will have to take the back entrance," whispered Calandra. "Can you swim?"

Scarlett wasn't amused. She nodded. One of her favourite ways to keep fit, if indeed she enjoyed keeping fit, was to swim, and in that regard she was a reasonably strong swimmer. But she looked down at the sea below and thought that it was an entirely different prospect to swimming there as to swimming in the pool. She was cold enough already before immersing herself into the waters around Scotland that she knew were never warm.

"They are all around here," whispered Calandra. "But I think that's because they know where we're going, I don't think they know where you are. The last time they just got lucky with the search after the dragon found us. They tracked the car...maybe, maybe not," pondered Calandra. "Too many maybes. Anyway, the main thing to do is don't dive headfirst. If you hit something with your feet at least you'll only break something fixable."

Scarlett looked at her in horror. "My head? As long as my head is okay? Are we going to jump in there?"

"Jump down there," said Calandra, "don't be so stupid. Break your legs in those rocks. Go another hundred metres back behind me, and then we'll jump from there."

Scarlett's heart danced a rollercoaster of emotions, at first delighted about not jumping into the sea where they were, and then horrified this woman thought jumping a hundred metres farther along would be any better. But what choice did she have? Her stomach knotted, and she could feel the panic rising. It was a hell of a drop down from the cliff.

Before she could think any further on it, Calandra grabbed her by the hand and they were running along the cliff edge. About a hundred metres further along, Calandra pushed her down into the snow and crouched alongside. Scarlett watched her head turn this way and that before she faced Scarlett and pointed at the sea. Scarlett looked at her in horror. Calandra stood up and Scarlett copied her automatically. Then, without warning, Calandra swept a hand under Scarlett's leg, another across her back and threw her off the cliff.

Scarlett fought not to scream, and it was only a few seconds later that that her body hit the icy cold water below. At first she panicked, as the chill ran through her. Her eyes were open, but she was struggling to see anything through the murky water. She needed to find a way to the surface, to get some air, but then a hand grabbed around her waist, and she turned and saw Calandra's face beside her. The woman was swimming hard with one hand and they made progress back towards the cliff they jumped from. As it was so blurred, Scarlett was not sure exactly how or what they entered through before she was thrust headfirst out of the water and onto a small beach. The beach was inside a cave which was lit up by a lamp some distance away. Scarlett stopped and tried to get her bearings, but Calandra was already on her feet trudging off towards the light.

"Come on then," said Calandra, her voice much more audible now. "This is only a small cave, it's time to go see a proper zoo!"

8

The Zoo

Scarlett followed Calandra along a narrow pass cut into the rock. On either side, the rock was black and wet, and it seemed to snake first left and then right. They walked for about three minutes before a sudden change took place and carpet appeared on the floor. The walls changed from rock to panelling, a deep mahogany wood. Scarlett felt she was entering a council from the 16th century. This panelling ran for a short distance before ending in a wooden door with brass fittings. There was a knocker in the centre of the door which could easily accommodate hands much larger than those of a human. Watching Calandra slam the knocker against the door with such venom, Scarlett wondered if she was going to break down the door. They then waited for a few minutes until they heard footsteps on the other side. The door swung open at an even pace.

Looking through the now open space, she saw a man of average height with neatly cut black hair and a trim beard. He was sitting in a wheelchair. Military medals adorned his chest and he wore a red dress jacket, black trousers and smart shoes. She watched the man give Calandra a swift nod before he turned and scanned Scarlett. There seemed to be a moment of worry before he nodded curtly and began to wheel himself backwards. Calandra strode off, and Scarlett decided she should just follow as no one was really indicating anything else. Passing through the wooden door, she heard it close.

"I heard footsteps," said Scarlett, "Is there anyone else around?"

"Generally, we like to introduce ourselves before asking such pertinent questions, and so without further ado, my name is Major MacDuff Lane, the keeper of this place. And I believe you are Miss O'Meara, erstwhile beast master, current source of the department's troubles." The man smiled somewhat disingenuously.

"I wouldn't say trouble."

"She's trouble," said Calandra. "Plenty of trouble."

"It's good to see you, Miss Calandra," said the Major, "but it has been a while now."

"It's was only the one time," said Calandra, "on the induction tour so to speak, but I didn't forget you."

Scarlett watched Calandra give the Major a somewhat angry look and turn her head away, flicking her black ponytail back towards him. The man seemed to smile and drink in this haughty view before spinning round on his wheels, moving further along the corridor ahead. He spoke over his shoulder as he moved deeper into the secret place.

"But it's good to have guests, especially such a fine pair of ladies. Of course, we can fix a drink for you, but if I recall, you were partial to the whisky last time. But as far as what our friend desires, if we need something special we can raid the cellar. Yes, it's good to get visitors, and the gang will be really pleased to see you."

"The gang?" asked Scarlett.

"He means the animals. The Major lives alone and keeps the zoo. But then there are good reasons for that, ain't there Major? I won't tell people any more, but you certainly didn't tell me."

"You may have regretted my attempt at a somewhat romantic liaison last time," said the Major in an even tone, "but I did not. Cannot blame a man for trying."

"I believe I did blame you last time," said Calandra. "And that bloody nose should have put you off forever."

"There was no need for that," said the Major roughly, "and we've another guest with us so let's behave. It's just around this corner, Miss O'Meara, but I believe the gang are already anticipating your arrival."

Scarlett could hear lots of noises coming along the corridor and there was genuine excitement as they turned the corner into a vast cavern. The panelling of the corridor broke away and the natural rock was left to provide the frame for this great expanse. Scarlett saw many animals held within a pen and some in open spaces loosely tied off. None of the creatures seemed normal but to be a combination of animals stuck together or something completely different. One thing that was obvious, however, was that all of the animals had noted their arrival, all intensely so, to the point that each one was standing at the very edge of their various pens looking right at her.

"So, drinks first," asked the Major, "or do we go straight into the tour?"

"I need that whisky," said Calandra. "I think you should get my friend one too. Couple of towels wouldn't go amiss either," she said. "Apologies for dripping over your carpet."

"It's waterproof," said the Major, "but it has been a while since anyone has come through that entrance."

Scarlett turned and looked fiercely at Calandra. "That entrance? You mean there's another one?"

"Oh, yes," said the Major, "there are numerous entrances. But she brought you through the gentle one."

Standing still in the vast cavern, Scarlett waited for the Major to return. Calandra was right about the towels, and Scarlett looked at the wet footprints she had left behind her. The Major then returned with a small round drinks tray attached to his wheelchair. Scarlett could see two whiskys with what appeared to be coloured umbrellas and fancy straws sticking out of them. She saw Calandra shake her head before grabbing a towel off the Major. Another one was thrust towards Scarlett.

"If you would turn around, Major," said Calandra.

"But of course," said the Major, "we're not Philistines here."

"More like a caveman," said Calandra and then smiled as she heard the Major snort. Without further ado, Scarlett watched Calandra strip to her underwear and dry herself off. She then walked to one side of the vast cavern they were in and stood against the wall. Scarlett watched but then undressed herself and began to dry. Calandra returned with what looked like decorators cover suits, disposable paper that people wore over the top of the clothing when painting. Calandra climbed into a suit and did it up before waiting for Scarlett to do the same. It felt like putting on some sort of waterproof sheet and she felt her skin go itchy at the feel of the material, but nonetheless, Scarlett was happy to be re-clothed and in something a little drier.

"We are good now, Major," said Calandra.

The Major turned his wheelchair and nodded, before handing the drinks to the women. Scarlett was taken aback by the number of umbrellas she had to remove before taking a sip of a coloured liquid.

"What's this?" asked Scarlett, her drink tasting very alcoholic.

"Just a little speciality knocked up for you," said the Major. "It's important to make guests welcome."

"But it's only you having one of those," said Calandra, "Careful, that may be part of the Major's arsenal."

"There's no need to put it that way," countered the Major, "but nonetheless a man can take a rebuke when he hears one."

"When he gets a bloody nose," laughed Calandra, looking at Scarlett with a smile.

"Indeed," said the Major. "If we can get to work."

The Major wheeled himself to a large area which was cordoned off by ropes. Inside was a creature with the neck of the giraffe but the markings of a zebra. It was ungainly due to its fat body on which were stubby webbed feet. Scarlett read the legend that was held on a plaque in front of the animal's pen. It was in another language, but Scarlett tried to see what letters she could make out. While she was staring at the writing, the animal came forward and dipped its neck. Its face came into view and it gently moved itself forward twisting its neck and moving its head with small ears onto Scarlett's bosom. Part of her wanted to jump away, unsure what this creature was doing. A tongue emerged to lick the side of her face. She felt herself begin to step back. But then another instinct took over, and she wrapped her arms round the creature, cuddling it into herself like she was embracing a child.

"I've never seen that" said the Major.

"Seen what?" asked Scarlett.

"The last time," said Calandra, "that thing nearly took my arm."

"Well if you do approach things in a manner in which I haven't stated, then bad things will happen."

"In a manner which you stated? You stated nothing, too busy looking at my behind."

Their bickering seemed to fade. Scarlett let the noise drift from her ears because another voice was taking prominence. It was not so much in words, but rather waves of emotions. *Warmth, friendliness, someone at last, she understands. Can they stay here? Would you stay here, as there's no one else here?* Scarlett could sense the creature's loneliness, could feel the sense of loss.

"It's the only one of its kind here," said the Major, continuing a sentence that Scarlett never heard the start of.

"And it doesn't want to be here," said Scarlett. "It doesn't want to be here, it's lonely. Where's the rest of its kind?"

The rest of its kind are still roaming the planes of its world. Sadly, we can't get to those planes at the moment."

Scarlett frowned. "What planes? Somewhere in Africa?"

"You've got quite a bit to learn," said Calandra. "One of the great things about working for the Agency are the exciting travel opportunities. Indeed, I'm not long back from somewhere dusty and dark. You never know what sort of people you're going to meet." The tone was sarcastic, heavily so.

"This fellow's home is a dimension away," said the Major. "Not having been there myself, the creature was brought back by Major Havers many years ago. In all fairness, the animal was being hunted, he probably saved its life."

"Doesn't seem to be appreciating that," Scarlett released her mind from the animal's and turned to take in the rest of the so-called zoo.

"Yes, yes," said the Major, "we should move on. So much to see."

"Very placid creature," said Scarlett.

"If you say so," said the Major, "but it took an intruder out before. That's why it's towards an entrance. It's been all right with me, but the intruder wasn't so lucky. Quick, though, the man went quick."

Scarlett felt a little uneasy and quickly turned her attention to the next animal. This cage was made of thick glass and the animal inside was green and slimy with at least five different eyes. *Watch this! Watch this!* The voice was just there in her mind, not through her normal hearing. The animal in front suddenly changed and this time it looked like a blackbird, with large talons of gold. Then a doglike creature. Some sort of slug. Now almost humanoid.

"Essential, that glass cage," said the Major, "if he got out we wouldn't have a clue what he was."

"I'm not good with the whole animals in cages thing," said Scarlett. "He doesn't seem that happy. He is desperate to show off."

"Yes, normally I'm fortunate to see a change every month."

He continued the tour, showing a multitude of different animals and each one responding to Scarlett in some way. It took a couple of hours to see all of the animals, especially since they all seemed to embrace Scarlett. Eventually the three left the large cavern, and the Major led them through to a slightly smaller cave which had a thin ledge and a lot of water beyond.

"This is our little aquarium," said the Major, "but we only have one guest. He can be quite rough, though, so I'd stay back."

At the far end of the water's surface Scarlett could see a tentacle emerging. It had suckers on the inside, like those of an octopus, but the colour of the limb was shocking pink. A head appeared in the centre of the water, and Scarlett met its eyes. Looking further down, she saw some of the sharpest teeth anyone should ever come across. There were seven more tentacles appearing now, razor like pieces of skin on the back of each tentacle. She was waiting to hear something, waiting for the animal to talk to her in that way the rest had, but there was nothing.

"This is quite a brute," said the Major, "we'll not stay here that long, but rather we'll retire downstairs where we can observe it under the water. Magnificent beast though. Capable of tearing apart some of the most fearsome creatures I've ever seen, it definitely has some sort of malignancy to it. Not really a creature you want to be in with."

There was a cool breath on the back of her neck. Scarlett felt hands on her shoulders. Those hands belonged to Calandra, the touch too cool through the thin fabric of her disposable outfit to be anyone else. She wondered why she'd come so close. As much as her nerves were already on edge with all she had seen, Scarlett was not prepared for what happened next. There was a shove, a very hard shove, and Scarlett fell face first into the water. She heard the Major's cry before a tentacle wrapped itself around her.

She felt like something was choking the life out of her and realised that a tentacle was wrapped around her neck. Another went around her waist and she was dragged through the water at high speed. Having always been one of those people who can open their eyes underwater, she opened them now, and she saw a few bubbles then some sharp teeth appear in front of her. The shoulder of her costume was ripping apart but that was the least of her worries as she realised she was in front of the eyes and the teeth belonging to the head of the creature. Trying to breathe, she only got water in her mouth for her efforts.

She needed to get clear, she needed to be away from this creature. Why was she thrown in? What was that woman doing? Well, she wasn't putting up with this, this was wrong. Scarlett felt her blood rising within, that petulant angry side her colleagues had laughed at. "Oh Madam's kicking off again," they had said, which had only made her more angry. But the rage was draining away any fear she had as every fibre of her being shouted *stop* at the creature in front.

Yes. The voice was laden with resentment. It felt like a reluctant servant had had to acquiesce to the demand. She felt the hold on her throat loosen and her waist began to feel less pain as it too was released from the grip of this creature. Relief washed over Scarlett, but then she realised that she was still under the water and still running out of breath. She turned to swim away but she was disorientated and unsure where the ledge and safety now lay. Her anger hadn't been dissipated and an idea came to her. *Put me back.* A tentacle grabbed round her waist, and she felt herself lifted out of the water. Gently, she was placed back on the ledge and the tentacle moved away. Before her, Calandra and the Major were staring right at her breastbone.

"What?" asked Scarlett, "What the hell was that?"

The Major simply stared in an unnerving fashion. Scarlett

realised apart from any remnants of disposable garment, she was basically in her underwear which the man seemed focused on. Calandra was maintaining a stare too but she stepped forward and her hand reached out to just above Scarlett's bosom. Scarlett slapped her hand away

"Get off. Fed up being this guinea pig you look at. And what the hell was that?"

"Really does work," said Calandra, "there's no way you should have been able to do that."

"What do you mean? Is it really that big a surprise I was able to talk to that beast, is that what this is all about?"

"It is a surprise," said the Major, "no one talks to that beast. No one gets near to it. That thing rose in the deep of another place and is feared by everyone. It has an evil running through it that usually only destroys. When its head rises above the water it's going to take you away. You don't hang around it."

"But you commanded it," Calandra said, "you made it put you back. You *are* a beast master. The other animals before, you could be some sort of trainer, but not with this thing, this is like the dragon."

"Dragon?" asked the Major, "What dragon? I don't have a dragon here."

"No, you don't. But we met one on the way, and this little lady managed to convince it to scarper."

"Only to put me down," said Scarlett.

"And then she did the same with this thing."

"No, she didn't," stated the Major in an even tone. "The dragon and this beast of the deep are very, very different. The dragon has an intelligence like us. This creature has none of that, it's very direct, it's very simple. It hunts. It destroys. There is no comparison."

Scarlett realised that they were saying all this while still looking straight at her breastbone. There was a heavy glow from her skin, so strong that it seemed to reach up to her shoulders and down to her waist. Calandra reached again towards Scarlett's breastbone and once again she slapped it away.

"If you don't mind, I'd like a towel. It's cold after being in the water," Scarlett said. "And kindly don't stare, Major."

Wheeling the chair away quickly, the Major returned with a towel which Scarlett wrapped around her. The Major had stopped his staring, but Calandra continued, watching the glow on Scarlett's breastbone.

"We'll go this way, ladies," said the Major. "Still plenty to see. The man deftly manoeuvred his chair around the women, leaving them behind him.

"You pushed me in," said Scarlett resentfully. "You knew that thing was a killer, you knew what it could do and yet you pushed me in. I nearly died in there, I nearly choked to death. What exactly were you going to do if I hadn't sorted it out myself?" She couldn't read Calandra. *One night she's like best pals and then this.*

"I wouldn't worry about that," said Calandra, "you're not the first blonde to need a chaperone."

9

Flame

There was an explosion of colour and feathers flew around the new room they had entered. The area had been accessed via a short corridor and a double set of screen doors presumably to keep the occupants in and not risk the mistake of a slightly open door. She could hear a myriad of voices in her head, each one seemingly more excited, and then there was the squawking that her ears could hear as well.

I should try to focus, she thought.

In the room, different birds came into sight, and Scarlett was astounded by the variety and the strangeness of some. It was true that most had wings of some sort, but there were thin necks and elongated beaks as well as short stubby birds, some with webbed feet. Some had the usual three to four digit splayed feet she saw in the birds of Britain, but there was actually one with feet as well, human feet. A sleek jet black bird flew overhead and she was sure she heard the word *hi.* Time and again, birds in greater number would start to touch or land on Scarlett.

"We certainly seem to have got the party going," said the

Major. "I haven't seen them like this, ever."

"They certainly don't want me," said Calandra. It was true, for all the noise that was going on with the sweeping back and forth of the birds, they stayed well away from Calandra. The Major held out in his hand, and a small bird landed on it. The bird twisted its head briefly before swooping around Scarlett in a friendly fashion.

"That's different," said the Major, "he normally sits with me quite happily. You really have their attention."

"All I did was walk in the room," said Scarlett. She was still wrapped up in a towel, feeling slightly cold. Her curiosity with the birds wasn't strong enough to stop her looking down on her breastbone which was aglow with the strongest light she had seen coming from the necklace. She wondered why this was, why the birds were so active. She closed her eyes.

Suddenly, she was swooping around the room, diving in and out, racing past the Major's head. This perspective changed again. She was swooping and gliding but in a different fashion, longer, more controlled. And then she was darting here and there, quick sudden movements. She knew she could get inside the heads of animals but with the birds it was so easy. Scarlett took her time jumping from bird to bird, studying the behaviour she had stepped into.

The Major seemed quite happy to let this happen, indeed he was quite aghast and somewhat excited. Calandra looked bored in the corner. With no birds coming to her, it seemed she had grown quickly tired of the flamboyant show by the feathered creatures.

"Put your arm out," said Scarlett.

The ice woman raised her eyebrows, but then Calandra did as she was told and extended a right arm. As she did so, she stood looking around because nothing seemed to be happening. Her arm moved down as if something had landed on it but there was nothing there. She looked around with squinting eyes to see if she could see anything. There was nothing. The Major started to laugh obviously aware of some joke Calandra wasn't. Scarlett smiled, and Calandra looked at her with eyes that seemed insistent that something was going to happen if somebody didn't tell her what was going on.

"Any feeling?" said Scarlett.

"I can feel him," Calandra said.

"It's not a him," said the Major.

Scarlett closed her eyes, and she could feel the bird becoming part of her. She looked into the face of Calandra. The woman's eyes were looking past her, looking at everyone else except at the viewpoint Scarlett now had. Scarlett moved the bird along her arm towards her head. The view turned, and she saw herself through the bird's eyes.

Do you want me to burn? We don't like to show ourselves. Over time we've become alone. I lost them.

I don't understand thought Scarlett. *What happened? Who did you lose?* There was an overwhelming sadness flooding through Scarlett at this time, melancholy she couldn't control. She burst into tears, going onto her knees at the sudden feeling of loss and grief. In the background, she heard the Major clapping like an excited schoolboy.

Can I come to you? Do I have to stay with this woman?

Rising up and standing upright, Scarlett let her arm move out straight. She felt the sudden weight of the bird. Then before her eyes, the bird suddenly appeared. It looked almost like a small eagle but was white throughout except for a red beak and tiny black eyes. The feet were pale limbs with red talons at the end, similar in colour to the beak, and Scarlett felt them grab into her arm just too tightly. Her flesh cut and small drops of blood started to drip onto the floor.

"I've only ever seen her appear twice," said the Major, "and that was in the early days. Sometimes I wondered if we'd lost her. But she always took the food."

The bird turned its head and looked straight at Scarlett who was becoming uneasy at the weight of the bird on her arm. As if anticipating the issue, the bird flew off and landed on her shoulder. Some of her wet blonde hair tangled up in the bird's feet, but again, its grip was so strong it drew blood off her shoulder. As if sensing something was wrong, the bird jumped off and sat on the ground. The Major moved over clapping wildly.

"Truly amazing, truly amazing. She's never gone to anyone like that to sit on. You really do have a way with them, don't you?" said the Major.

"It keeps talking to me whenever it lands anywhere. I know it wants to be with me but this isn't going to work," said Scarlett.

"Maybe you were just a better nest than most," said Calandra. "I think we need to get you some leathers."

Yes, came the thought, *something for your skin, something so I can sit on you, without hurting something.* Scarlett slowly moved forward with her hand and stroked the belly of the creature. She felt discomfort almost immediately. *Yes,* Scarlett thought, *an independent soul. You're not somebody's little pet. That was the Major's mistake. He sees a pet and that's why you don't appear. There, that's a lesson he will have to find out for himself. What do they call you, what's name works for a gorgeous bird like you? Snowy? Sounds a bit too cuddly. What name is elegant enough, what name fits something as stunningly elegant as you?*

I do have a name, came the reply. *Flame is what they call me, or is what they could call me. I guess no one has been able to call it for so long.*

"Flame," Scarlett said. "She's called Flame."

"Amazing," said the Major, "just amazing. I do hope that you know what she was."

"What do you mean?" said Scarlett. "She just told me her name, it's Flame."

The Major grinned, happy to still have knowledge to deliver. "It's Flame, well at least she says it's Flame. I never knew that, but she has a flame, she's a firebird. I've only seen it in the early days. But once she starts, the fire and flames come on. Just amazing that," said the Major, "just downright amazing." He took a short breath. "That sounds like HQ is trying to contact us."

Scarlett noticed that Calandra was nodding, but she couldn't hear anything. The Major indicated that they needed to go, commenting they could just leave the birds for now and come back later. Scarlett watched the Major turn his wheelchair around and followed him out of the room, Calandra taking up the rear. Scarlett tried not to show any discomfort as she felt something invisible land on the shoulder and cling on. The bird apologised, but was obviously too attached to just remain behind. Scarlett give herself an inner smile, happy in the knowledge that she seemed a little more in tune with certain things than these so-called experts around her.

They were led along various corridors until the party of three came into a room with large screens and basic furniture around chairs and desks. Most of the desks were bare, here in the tidiest office Scarlett had ever seen. Blue screens were flashing, and Scarlett stood in front of one before seeing a keypad beneath the screen. The Major wheeled himself to the pad, keyed in a number and then the screen in front of Scarlett lit up. Wilson appeared. He was dressed smartly, sitting at his office with the large view but with a countenance that was slightly worried. In the background, Scarlett saw the working office she had left so very recently.

"Good to see you, Miss Calandra, Major, sorry to cut short your trip, but there's been an issue with Rodriguez. Major give us a moment." The Major excused himself and then wheeled away.

Calandra's face narrowed. "What issue?"

"Mr. Rodriguez was sent to investigate certain lines of enquiry around the necklace. As he was conducting those enquiries he went missing. Despite our efforts, we have been unable to ascertain his whereabouts other than he went missing in the Swiss Alps. I'll send you the last co-ordinates we had for him. I'd send someone else, but the local agents are not aware of the necklace's existence, and although relatively new to the organisation, you know Rodriguez's movements better than anyone else. I want you to go to these coordinates and find him, find what he knows. Bring him back if you can. If not, then I'm authorising you to pick up the line of enquiry and find out who is behind the search for this necklace. I'll send the details on the secure link so you can scan them before you go. But I want you on the way in the next half-hour."

Calandra nodded. "There's a problem. They know we are here with the Major."

"You'll have to just keep ahead. They must have traced you when you left, so they must have some awareness of how we move about. Don't take company transport. Where possible, use normal methods and keep it very low key. As for Miss

Scarlett, she's probably best with you, clear of the organisation if they are seeing our response. Anyway, I think she might be an asset."

"She's right here in the room," said Calandra, "but I'm not sure she's going to take to being an asset."

Scarlett marched in front of the screen. "Been swimming?" asked Wilson. "I see you've made a friend." Calandra spun round and looked at Scarlett. It was then that she nodded to herself, content that Wilson was correct.

"You hear her too?" asked Scarlett.

"Nothing so advanced, but it's quite obvious from the indentation in the shoulder that something is there, and as I recall, the only creature we have that can go invisible and which is that large is the firebird. I'd advise you to be very careful as she is quite a dangerous animal."

But in her head came another voice asking Scarlett, *Is he talking about me?*

Yes, said Scarlett, *he says you're dangerous.*

He's right.

"So you can talk to her as well," said Wilson. Scarlett realised she must have been quiet for too long, but she simply nodded her head in reply. "I'd love to stay and chat, unfortunately, we don't have time as Miss Calandra and you need to be on the road. I suggest leaving your feathered friend behind. Miss Calandra, the moment you leave, you go dark. I don't expect an update, if I need one, I'll find you."

The screen went blank.

"So we're leaving then," said Scarlett.

"Obviously," muttered Calandra. "He seems somewhat distracted."

"Is it serious? Is Rodriguez in trouble?"

"Rodriguez is probably dead," said Calandra, "and I'm about to take you into the middle of this. Yes, it's kind of serious."

The door at the far end of the room burst open, and the Major wheeled himself in. He caught the expression on Calandra's face and asked what happened. She was sullen and said nothing except to ask about ways out and that they were leaving in five minutes. The Major described a route that seemed rather strange to Scarlett but then she thought it was probably code.

"As we're leaving," said Scarlett, "would it be possible to get me some clothing? I don't think it's going to be wise to walk around in a towel in the Swiss Alps."

The Major muttered a cheap line about how she would look great in anything, before wheeling himself out of the room to return some minutes later with Scarlett's and Calandra's clothes which were now dry. Changing quickly, she watched Calandra go to a terminal and swiftly read something on it. Calandra turned back, still grim faced, with a look of determination on it.

"When is the train, Major?" asked Calandra, now changing quickly herself.

"I believe you need to be there by three o'clock. There's a number of beaches and coves you could alight on and then send the little lady back to me. Take care of my transport going in and out of here as well."

Scarlett wondered what on earth they were on about, but she knew she'd be facing something different again. The Major wheeled himself out of the door. Calandra followed, and Scarlett hurried so as not to get lost in the complex. The Major took them through more corridors until they re-entered one with wood panelling, similar to that corridor that had been the prelude to this whole zoo. At the end of the corridor, once again, was the accursed small beach and water. The difference was the black object sitting on the beach, about the size of a small car. It seemed to have fins on it, and a screen at the front.

"She's ready," said the Major. "Don't get her damaged."

"Don't worry," said Calandra throwing the Major a look, "You'll see her again. Scarlett was sure that the Major winced when Calandra shook his hand but he brightened up and extended a hand towards Scarlett.

"Been an absolute pleasure, my dear. You really are quite remarkable."

Scarlett wasn't quite sure how to take this. She noticed his eyes rolling over her figure. It was like being patronised by some estranged uncle, like you were his little doll. "I mean, with the birds of course," said the Major. "You're quite remarkable with the birds."

The pause between the end and the start of the sentence was too long. Calandra was already climbing into the vehicle on the beach. Seeing the top slid back, Scarlett rushed from her awkward moment, ran up to the vehicle as best as she could and jumped in beside Calandra. There was a dashboard of lights, switches and a solid joystick in front of each of the two seats inside.

"I thought Wilson told you to leave the bird behind."

"Well, he's not my keeper. How did you know?" asked Scarlett.

"I didn't. I really need to teach you poker," said Calandra with a slight grin on her face. She flicked several switches in the car. Scarlett could see the Major watching them from the edge of the beach as the vehicle moved backwards into the water slipping down beneath the water. It was dark until lights illuminated the bay, and Scarlett could see rock all around her. The vehicle was comfy but tight and Scarlett could feel the firebird sitting against her legs in the foot well.

"Before we go, I think you need to be aware," said Calandra. "When we get back into the open, there is no more safely. If they followed us here, they will continue to hunt us. Whatever happens, don't hesitate. Do not think twice if you have to kill to save yourself. If you need an animal to do something, you do it. You may not have the training, you might not have the background in this, but trust me, if you want to survive from here on in, go full on with everything you've got."

"You don't get it," said Scarlett, "you talk like I know what I'm doing with this. You talk as if I'm in charge of these animals."

"But you are," said Calandra, "You sent the dragon away. You took control of that sea creature. Why do you think we were here? You think Wilson just wanted you to have a little time with the animals? No, we had to see if you are the real deal. And you are! Trust me, when you pile into a war, you've got to take every weapon you own with you and be prepared to use it."

"You think I'm in charge of this. You talk as if I know what I'm doing. This is all new to me. This is something I can't fully control, something I fully don't understand and you just expect me to use it."

"You think I understand this?" Calandra lifted her left arm and let the jacket sleeve drop up to elbow. Scarlett watched the hand go from the pure white flesh to almost glass in an instant. "I don't get this," said Calandra. "I never asked for it. It has killed people I love at my own hand. I am the Ice Maiden. You're a beast master. Live with it!"

10

The Train

The trip in the underwater vessel was long and uneventful. As there was little to see through the often murky water, Scarlett found herself reaching out to any fish that passed by. At one point, she tried to read an entire shoal of some type of fish, but the noise from the thoughts was unintelligible and overwhelming. Throughout the trip, Scarlett had no idea where they were going other than underwater.

Calandra was quiet for most of the trip, only occasionally taking a sip from the drinks that were inside the vehicle. There were several bottles of water to keep thirst at bay as the inside of the vessel was humid. Given the lack of enthusiasm for conversation, Scarlett found herself drifting away to eventually be overtaken by sleep. When she awoke they were still underwater and the dials and screens in front of them remained bright. Calandra was asleep.

Scarlett looked closely at the screens and tried to identify where she was. There was a moving map showing trenches and ridges, but Scarlett struggled to ascertain the vessel's location.

She saw a switch beside the map screen and reached forward to touch it. A hand shot out and grabbed her wrist.

"Don't touch anything," said Calandra, "We'll be there shortly. Just try and get a bit of rest."

"Sorry," said Scarlett. She took to looking back out the window, but it remained murky. Her mind drifted back to all that had happened, and she realised that part of her dreams had come true. This was an adventure, this was action, even if it was on the deadly side. She loved it when she could talk to the different creatures, but being grabbed and then pulled underwater by an octopus, being half drowned, being thrown off sides of cliffs, having dragons roll her car, that was all a little bit too much adventure at times.

She looked down at her top and saw the necklace glowing slightly underneath the skin. This means I have to cover up forever otherwise people will see this item that had taken over her life. Could she make its glow disappear? She watched through her top as the item seemed to resonate to her thoughts and began to dim. Was it gone? Scarlett pulled her top forward and looked straight down. There was no sign of light at all. She searched inside her top with her hands. There was nothing. All the fidgeting was of such a level that Calandra began to stir.

"What are you doing?" asked Calandra.

"It's not there anymore, it seems to have disappeared."

Calandra held up her hand. It was a pale white. Scarlett watched it turn glassy so that she could see through it. And then it was back to pale white flesh.

"It took time, but I have learnt to control it. It will be the same with you."

"What do you mean the same with me?"

"You learn to be a freak. You learn to control it. But it will drive everyone around you away, trust me. The abilities are very exciting, but in the end, you just end up alone."

"What do you mean? Bloody hell, you can attract guys, no problem."

"The attraction is not a problem," said Calandra, "It's just that I kill them."

"Kill them? Do you really mean kill them? Isn't that a bit extreme?"

Calandra raised her eyebrows and lay back in her seat. "I am a bit extreme," she said. "I'm surprised you hadn't realised that yet. Didn't you spot these freakish powers of ours?"

"But you turn to ice. Guys would love that."

"Not when you end up killing them."

"How?" she asked and Scarlett saw a tear forming.

"I lost one at my own hand and the other doesn't belong to me, he's somebody else's. But I killed what we had." A little shard of ice fell from her face.

"But at least you got your looks in the first place," said Scarlett. "You're in such great shape, they must fall at your feet."

Calandra looked at her, staring hard.

"Trust me, that doesn't count for much. I mean, look at you. It's not like you can't attract them yourself. But I bet you pick the losers. You grab whatever attention you can from a guy. You could do with a bit more pride. And a bit less anger."

Scarlett was about to react but there was too much truth in what was being said so she just lay back in her seat, closed her eyes and tried to get back to sleep. It must have worked because she was awoken suddenly by an alarm. In front of her, a light was flashing on the panel. Calandra was awake at the controls of the vessel.

"We'll be surfacing soon," said Calandra, "Get yourself together as it will soon be time to head out. Be ready to go."

"Go where? Where are we going to be going?"

"France, a little town in France where we will board a train. We'll get the train into Paris and from there to Switzerland."

"Switzerland? I've never been to Switzerland."

"Well, it's cold mountains at this time of year. I'm sure you'll love the scenery."

The craft broke through the water onto the beach, barely sticking out above the waves, and Calandra pushed a button to open the top which allowed the women to exit. They looked rather strange in their dark outfits as they walked across the beach in the morning light. There was no one around. Scarlett turned to see the vessel behind them closing up and disappearing back under the water. Calandra walked in silence, constantly on guard, and Scarlett followed. They had no backpack, no luggage. Scarlett wondered where anything was going to come from. She wasn't carrying any cash. They had no British currency nor euros, not even a credit card.

The road to the station was deserted, and they stepped aboard a train five minutes later. Calandra produced a slim wallet from inside of her jacket when the ticket man asked to see their tickets. Still on their guard, they sat back on the train. It took about an hour to reach Paris where the station was a busy mass of people. Calandra purchased tickets for a sleeper train that would pass through to Switzerland by the following morning. Feeling famished, the women had lunch at a quiet cafe a few streets away from the station. Once they picked up the sleeper train, they retired to their cabin which had one bed above the other and a window to look out of.

"Is it still with you?" asked Calandra.

"Is what still with me?"

"The bird. The one that seemed to cling to you, the invisible one."

"I don't think so," said Scarlett but hesitantly as she became aware of something almost like a slight tickling across her cheek. She felt something move off her shoulder and then there on the bed, the bird suddenly revealed itself. "Where did that come from?" asked Scarlett

"I knew she wouldn't be far," said Calandra. "You two seem to have a connection. She doesn't want to leave you. You really didn't know she was there?"

"No," said Scarlett. "I didn't have a clue."

I'm always here with you, came the reply in her thoughts. *Where are we going?* Scarlett thought back at the bird. *Don't worry about where we're going, just stay close.* Soon after, the bird's small black beady eyes pierced her with their gaze before the bird turned in a whirlwind of feathers intended to mark its annoyance at the answer. *No need to be like that.* Scarlett reached over and smoothed the bird's feathers.

"I'm tired," said Calandra. "It was a lot of driving, so I'm going to catch some sleep. I'll take the top bunk if you don't mind."

Scarlett nodded, and she watched Calandra strip down before jumping into the bed at the top. It wasn't long before she heard some light snoring. Feeling something alight onto her shoulder, Scarlett moved to the window to look out. All this rushing about, Scarlett realised, meant that she hadn't really seen anything as they travelled. Then again, they weren't here to sightsee. Something was up with Rodriguez, and despite Calandra's even tone, she was clearly worried. Scarlett wondered if Calandra would rather have gone on the mission alone rather than babysitting Scarlett as she conducted her investigation. But that wasn't their call, and Scarlett didn't want other people to look after her. And then she wondered how many of them could turn to ice.

The journey was uneventful, and the dull view passed quickly. Calandra slept for a lot of the time, and Scarlett sat on her bed chewing over thoughts while the bird sat on the bed beside her. But she wasn't great company, and the bird took the hint. Scarlett didn't want to talk, or at least think. Outside the train rumbled on into Switzerland, and Scarlett saw the scenery rising up around them.

Presently, there came a knock at the door and someone spoke with what seemed like a French accent. Scarlett couldn't work out what had been said, but Calandra said something back. She then hung down from the bed above.

"Did you hear anything?"

Scarlett shook her head and soundlessly Calandra dropped to the floor below, quickly pulling on her clothing. After putting Scarlett to the back of the little cabin, towards the window, she opened the door gently. There was a man in a train guard's uniform holding a tray in front of them. Looking first at Calandra, he then seemed to search round the little cabin with his eyes before settling them on Scarlett. Calandra, without hesitation, launched a kick to his midriff, sending him back into the train carriage before spinning round to face Scarlett. Scarlett heard the glass break behind her and was grabbed by the neck. She was off her feet and being pulled out the window.

The next thing she knew, she was on top of the train being held by various arms. The wind was rushing past, and she thought she would fly off the train but such was the hold that she remained motionless. Despite the wind and noise, she could hear the commotion down below and imagined that Calandra was dealing with being attacked herself. She heard a cry. Not that of a human, but that of a bird.

There was a loud screech by her right hand side, and she saw a blur pass by her, a rapid motion of feathers and clawed feet. Flame was taking on her name and was now ablaze. The creature swooped down, knocking whatever was holding Scarlett off to one side, and she slid across the train before grabbing onto the edge. Her legs dangled over and with every fibre of her being, she held on tight, praying she could get back into the carriage. Her fingers were slipping. The window beneath her smashed open, and she heard the cry of a man falling. This made Scarlett panic, resulting in her grip loosening and she began to fall off the carriage. She felt a cold hand grabbing her and pulling her back inside.

Falling on the floor, she felt a leather boot hold her there and looking up she saw the frame of Calandra, black leather jacket, black jeans and a face that was now ice. She was clearly keeping people at bay with a long pole. The train compartment was extremely tight, but she seemed to be able to move and strike effectively with a force that belied the space available.

"We need to go," said Calandra and the boot was lifted off Scarlett and a hand reached down picking her up onto her feet.

"Yes," Scarlett said "But where? We're on a moving train."

"Behind me, down the corridor. Just go."

Scarlett didn't hesitate, turned and ran. The carriages were one endless corridor of cabins off to the right with all of the doors shut. Scarlett raced forward, making it through several carriages before she turned round to see if Calandra was following. She wasn't there. Scarlett was looking back down the corridor when one of the cabins opened, a hand grabbed her, and she was pulled inside the cabin door which shut behind her.

She was thrown onto the bed and then she felt a figure looming over. Although it was dark, she could make out the shadow over her, and she knew it was that person again. Person…thing…whatever it was.

"You are like your mother, petulant, always fighting, always resisting. Your friends are not here now, so we will be able to talk and understand each other a lot better." The voice was sinister, threatening. Scarlett felt herself pinned in a most uncomfortable way. It was like a knee was pushed down on her chest, her hands were held and the breath of this thing came around her neck. She felt that he was almost, if indeed it was a he, looking over her, enjoying. Her flesh crept. She began to fight back against the restraint.

"It will not do you any good," said the figure, "I know you like it, know as I knew your mother. But you'll submit. Unlike her, you'll submit. Otherwise, you'll have to end it all."

Scarlett felt cold and angered at the thought of her mother doing something because of this figure. She tried to fight back, but her hands were held tight, and she endured the breath as it moved across her face. It felt like an unwanted approach from one of those drunks that she used to endure in her late teens because she was out at the nightclub. They always felt you were somehow easy. But she wouldn't be. But then it dawned on her that her own strength may not be enough. She went to yell but a hand clamped her mouth. Scarlett fought back tears as she felt this figure move over the top of her. *Flame, where are you Flame?* The window of the cabin exploded and it felt like the room went on fire. There was a cry from the figure as it tumbled off her, and she saw stood over her a flaming bird and yet, when it touched her, it wasn't hot to her.

But the figure had recovered and reached out towards the flame. The bird cried, turned and shot out of the window. The figure looked wounded and Scarlett didn't wait to make sure. She dived headlong out of the train window. Crashing down a bank, she tumbled into undergrowth. Her legs whipped into the ground and she was sure that she must have broken her ankle. As she continued down, she covered her head with her arms which felt severely bruised when she stopped rolling. She didn't move. She heard the train disappear past. Opening her eyes, she saw Flame in front of her, large talons on show. *Thanks,* she thought at the bird. *You saved me.* There seemed a nod of the head, like an acknowledgement, but she wasn't sure. Flame turned, looking haughtily to the sky.

She knew she needed to move, she didn't know where to go. The bird took to the air, circling round for a time before coming back and flew lower around Scarlett before heading off in a direction. She picked herself up, checked that everything seemed to work, and she wandered off after the bird. Wandering across a field, she saw in the distance snow-covered mountains. Where would she go when she had no money? She couldn't tell a tale of this flaming bird looking after her or even what she was doing here. On reaching the end of the field, she started to feel down and out. She was stuck, and there was no one around except the bird. Too late, she saw that there was something else with her.

It was the same arm that had grabbed her in the train and pulled her to the ground. Looking up, she saw what appeared to be a man but he had at least six different limbs coming from the side of his body and the two legs he was standing on.

Shocked into inaction, she just stood there with her arms involuntarily folded around her. *Flame, where are you?* She saw another arm wrapped around the bird and then in her mind screams from the bird in pain assaulted her. The thing with the arms in front of her didn't speak. It didn't make a sound at all but began to lift her off the floor and carry her away. Then she heard a cry. It was female. It was livid. It was the voice of Calandra.

A long wooden stick struck down onto the limbs of the attacker, and Scarlett felt herself drop. From a prone position, she saw Calandra fend off the various arms one at a time before moving closer to the central body of the figure and then driving a stick under its chin, throwing it backwards. Then, as the figure regrouped, Calandra struck it across the cheek and turned round, almost losing balance. Remarkably two black wings shot out from Calandra's back and she rounded causing one of the wings to sweep the figure aside. The figure regrouped and was knocked to the floor again by the staff. This time it turned and fled.

Calandra turned back to Scarlett who couldn't contain the look of surprise on her face. Scarlett breathed in and out heavily as she saw Calandra standing there, large wings fully erupted from her back, standing in the moonlight, like the proud warrior that she was.

"I'd love to explain, but I have to say this again, it's time to go!"

11

What Rodriguez Found

The names that adorned the shops along the street of the small hamlet were lost on Scarlett as she knew no Swiss. Although Calandra seemed sure of where she was going, she was clearly on edge, the attack on the train having taken her by surprise. The openness of using such strange creatures was hard to grasp. Scarlett felt the comfort of the firebird on her shoulder, invisible though it was, it was a protective presence. The devotion of Flame in driving away the dark shadow that had attacked her more than made up for the occasional talon that broke the skin.

Then there was Calandra, now with black wings. Scarlett wondered what other surprises she would conjure over and above her obvious prowess with weapons. *I wonder where these people came from because back on the council estate in Wales there was no one like that next door. Yes, there are plenty of strange people in life but generally most people are ordinary folks living ordinary lives. This is a completely different world. In fact, it could be a completely different world some of these creatures came from.* She momentarily paused to consider this and thought, *Yes, I hope it's a completely different world.*

There was snow just above the hamlet on the mountainside, but the road itself was clear. The morning was in full swing and the sunlight felt good too, even if Scarlett was finding it all a bit chilly. Needless to say, Calandra, of course, didn't feel the cold and seemed more agitated by what was going on around them. She pointed to what looked like a dispensary over the road, and the pair crossed before opening the door resulting in a clatter of small chimes. A man appeared behind the counter which was stacked with medicines. He said something, in presumably Swiss. Scarlett had no clue, and she could see that Calandra was struggling as well. From Calandra's awkwardness, she concluded that this was not her first language, nor her second.

"Where's Austerley when you need him?" said Calandra under her breath. And then she replied to the gentleman behind the counter who seemed to concentrate quite hard on what she was saying. He gave a gentle nod and a shrug of the shoulders as if he had given them all he could. After seeming to wish everyone a good day, he went back into the store behind him. Calandra indicated it was time to go. Once they reached the sunshine outside, Scarlett tapped Calandra on the shoulder.

"Where are we going? Did he say anything useful? Did he know anything about Rodriguez? Gosh, I wish I had taken Swiss in school…"

"Shush! Don't say his name. The people that may have done away with him will know his name. Don't bring it up." Calandra paused for a moment and added, "And there's no such thing as a Swiss language. He was speaking in Romansh."

"Sorry. My first time as an international spy," said Scarlett.

"Okay. I'm just a little on edge. How did they find us? I was dark and then they showed up. Just a little worried as to how they did that. When I go dark, the company struggles to find me."

"Just what is *the* company that you work for?"

"That I work for? I think you'll find we both work for them. Is this just your idea of fun?" Calandra took Scarlett off the street to one side and then in a hushed tone said, "We work for SETAA."

"What's SETAA?"

"Not so loud. You understand it's secret, it doesn't exist. The Supernatural and Elder Threat Assessment Agency. We find the things from out of this world that are coming into this world, and we try and send them back to where they came from. And occasionally, we have to go somewhere out of this world to stop them. It's not the most glamorous life, but you do get to meet a lot of very strange people and things. Like me."

"You definitely are strange," said Scarlett, "but then again, you haven't got people running around trying to get hold of something on your chest."

"I could make an answer to that, but I won't," laughed Calandra. "The boys would like you. You have a way with words, and you certainly have heart. Yeah, the boys would like you."

"The boys?" asked Scarlett.

"Just the team I was on last," said Calandra. "I haven't worked with Rodriguez that long. Before that I was working with Mr. Austerley who you may have heard mentioned. He's deeply immersed in these things that we find strange and bizarre. In fact, he's often more bizarre than they are. And then there was

Kirkgordon. But he was just…" The silence didn't stop.

Scarlett wondered whether to reply, but she saw again the tear forming in Calandra's eye, a tear that never ran down the cheek but was merely crunched away by rapidly closing eyes. "Someone special?"

"Very special," said Calandra, "One of these men that matters to you above all other men. But I nearly killed him and nearly killed his wife, so I went away, kept away so that I didn't hurt those that were close anymore. It doesn't pay to get closer when you are this weird."

"Does that go for me too?" asked Scarlett. "Should I stay away from people?"

"Just remember, the closer they are, the more you hurt them. That's the dark side of being gifted."

"But what dark side?" asked Scarlett, "What exactly is my dark side?"

"I don't know, yet," Calandra said, "But there is always a dark side, and maybe the dark side in us brings out the worst in them. I saw a friend steal someone's foot because he could and he needed a foot. These gifts don't always do you any favours, sometimes they will bring you down."

Scarlett nodded and then looked around. "Okay, where is our friend?"

Calandra scanned the area before pointing off to the far end of the village. Together they walked, ignoring the calls of a posse of young men. *They're looking at me as well* thought Scarlett but she didn't have the nerve to look back to check if she was right. *No, they must have been, obviously.*

Calandra suddenly stopped in the middle of the street, turned to the left and looked up the mountainside to where there was a dwelling. She indicated for Scarlett to follow, and she strode up the incline. Scarlett tried hard to keep up, but her shorter frame wasn't built the same, and she eventually gave up. When Calandra reached the top, she turned around and gave Scarlett a rebuking glance, indicating she should have worked harder to catch up.

The house had two levels, and on the first floor was a balcony which had its curtains drawn. Calandra tried the front door but it was locked, and she turned to see if anyone was on the street below. Seeing it was clear, she jumped up, grabbing the underside of the balcony and spun herself up and onto it. Scarlett stood amazed and decided that whatever happened, she was not trying it as well. A few seconds later, Calandra opened the front door.

"Get the bird to go and sit on top of the house, let us know if anyone arrives."

Scarlett nodded, and she thought the instructions to the bird who responded. Scarlett never saw the bird leave her shoulder, but she was no longer weighed down. *Maybe I'm getting the hang of this beast master thing. It's all about understanding how to run the relationship, just a good job that it was so obedient, so ready to serve.*

Inside the house was decorated sparsely, and Calandra strolled around it, lifting up items, checking behind furniture, but seemed to be drawing a blank. Scarlett looked around too but was reluctant to touch anything in case she dropped it and put it back somewhere that wasn't correct. Calandra began shaking her head, and it was obvious she couldn't find anything. She reopened the front door, stepped outside, looked around and then came back in.

"What is it?" asked Scarlett.

"He was here," said Calandra, "The mark on the front of the

house says he was here, but there's no other sign at all. There's nothing. I can't seem to see anything."

"I can sense something," said Scarlett, "There's a presence here."

"Presence? What do you mean by presence?"

"Tapping into something, something is there. Hang on." Scarlett focused, pushing outward with her mind, and suddenly she could see down what appeared to be a corridor which was extremely dark. Little shards of light came in here and there, but otherwise, it was very dark. She scuttled forward, yes scuttled, which was a weird sensation. It was then she began to understand. She halted and looked around, forcing the head of whatever she was looking through down. Gasping at the large drop, she saw lots of boxes. She retreated from the mind she had been occupying.

"There's something under the floor. I was in a rat, and I could see it, a big drop with a box at the bottom, or maybe a case or papers or something. Something that looked important."

"You were inside a rat?" said Calandra. "It's gonna be below."

She took her staff, spun it hard into the wooden floor beneath them. The floor cracked, and Calandra began to break the floorboards apart until there was nothing below, just a concrete base. Moving into the next room, Calandra repeated the action but when she broke through this time, there was a small item located in a pit dug into the floor. The small pit was seemingly formed within the concrete base and wasn't a new addition. There was a mark on the box and it seemed to bring delight to Calandra's face.

"Rodriguez, this is Rodriguez's stuff, got his mark on it. We need to look at this."

Calandra lifted the box out of the floor and placed it on the floorboards beside her. It had a lock on it which Calandra ignored and instead placed a hand on the box. A deep cold seeped from her onto the box and lock. The lock expanded and broke, and Calandra opened the lid of the box.

Scarlett placed her hand inside to grab some papers she saw in the box, but it felt like she was reaching into a freezer. Nonetheless, she retrieved the paper. It appeared old and fragile with a few holes in it. She unfolded the paper and caused a slight rip.

Calandra muttered "be careful" beneath her breath. She looked at the script before shaking her head and tried to trace some figures in the air but nothing seemed to make sense. Scarlett took a look but she was bamboozled.

"We need to get these to Wilson. In fact, we need to get these to Austerley, he'll know what to do." She folded up the paper and tucked it inside her jacket. Calandra stood up, walked to the front of the house, and peered out of the window. Unsure what to do now, Scarlett followed her but was pulled aside.

"Far side, just behind the bush," said Calandra, "At least three of them. They were house watching, dammit. Should be assessing, so they should be alone."

"Does that mean this paper stuff is a setup?" asked Scarlett.

"No, with Rodriguez's mark on it we have to assume that what's written on that is important. The key thing at the moment is to get out of here with this paper and get it to Austerley. I need to get a phone."

How much time do we have?" asked Scarlett. "There's only three of them over there so you can take them on? You seem pretty handy with your staff."

"There's only three we have seen. Finding a phone is our best option so we know where to go when we run. Is the bird still on the roof?"

Scarlett reached out to the firebird with her mind. *Yes, I'm still here.* Scarlett nodded at Calandra.

"Good, then it can warn us when they come. Gotta make a phone call first."

The women searched the house, and Calandra located the telephone. She picked up the receiver, heard the dial tone, and quickly pressed some buttons.

"Is that Austerley's number?" asked Scarlett.

"No, it's just a number, and it will find him. Don't ask how or why. It's a technical thing, and they didn't tell me how it worked. But they did tell me if I rang this number, it would work wherever I am in the world."

There was a bit of a commotion outside, and Calandra handed Scarlett the phone.

"Tell Austerley everything that's happened, asking where to meet up and remember everything he says." Calandra turned away but then turned back. "And if he's being an arse, just give his ego a kick."

Scarlett placed the phone to her ear. There was a voice on the other end.

"Hello? Who the hell is this? This mobile working?"

"Hi, it's me, Scarlett."

"Scarlett? Who the hell's Scarlett? I told you people in the lab before, don't call me on this line. It's a secure line. You need to call me on a normal phone."

"I don't work for any lab, and I'm calling you because Calandra said so." The other end of the line went quiet before there was a quick intake of breath, and the man with the gruff voice responded.

"I don't know Cally. And who the hell are you again?"

"Yes, you do, and I'm Scarlett O'Meara. I am with Calandra, we're in Switzerland and she has some papers she needs you to look at to work out what they say. She asked me to ask you where to meet."

"You're not getting me with that one. I'm hanging up."

"No, no, no! Don't do that! Calandra is here, we need your help."

"If Calandra is there, then put her on the damn phone. Get her to speak to me herself."

"I'll try. Not sure if she'll come," said Scarlett.

"Why? What's up?"

Scarlett looked out the front window. "She seems to be in a bit of a fight, although to be fair, she's doing rather well."

"She's a beautiful creature. Amazing what she can do, the way she can adapt her body to almost any situation."

Scarlett was quite unsure what to make of that, wondering if he meant her figure or her ability. "Where do we meet?" she asked.

"*Nebulos categorical exposition of Kazern*. That's the book you want. That and *Schroder's phantasmal extrodinare*."

"What the hell does that mean?" asked Scarlett. "Are you some sort of joker? I'm in the middle of a deadly game, maybe about to be taken apart by some rather nasty things, and all you can do is spout this gibberish at me?"

The phone went dead and Scarlett was still holding the earpiece. It took a conscious effort to put it down, and she remembered what Calandra had said. *What had he said?* Desperately, she tried to remember, but her train of thought was broken by a man flying through the window of the house, shattering the glass and crashing into the sofa beside. She turned to kick him, but he was obviously out cold.

A head emerged with a black ponytail through the window and shouted "Out here, now!" Scarlett ran to the door, opened it and came face-to-face with what she could only describe as a man with a fire on his arm. It was ablaze with fire, and then he turned, and she could see his entire back was ablaze, and he started to roll down the hill. Scarlett saw the firebird swooping around in front of her, a beacon of protection as she saw many individuals climbing the hill in front of the house.

It was a tide of horror coming up the hill. Scarlett sought to see Calandra, and then she saw her black wings unfurled and the staff spinning. The creatures were flying left and right but still the tide was overflowing Calandra. As if she knew Scarlett was watching, she turned and shouted, "Run! Just run!"

"But the paper? Austerley?" shouted Scarlett.

"The bird! Send the bird to me!"

Go to her, bring back the paper. Bring back what she gives you.

Everything below was running up the hill when Scarlett turned and headed up the mountainside where the ice began to appear at her feet in abundance. *Ice and snow, great.* As she ran, she could hear flames crackling and cries from those who got too close to the firebird. Not being that fit, Scarlett found herself having to drive her legs with all she had up the steep mountain. As she entered the deeper snow, her legs howled at her, and she screamed back at them to move. Running seemed to be becoming a way of life, a way of life she wasn't happy with. A hand grabbed her foot, and she tumbled to the ground. Turning around to see her would-be attacker, she saw a man with an elliptical head, and she cried out as he reached forward. There was a sharp yell from the man, and he dropped down to the ground beside her, on fire. Scarlett rolled over, forcing her mind to stay away from the horror she just witnessed, forcing her body to pick itself up and run again.

Seeing a number of goats up the mountainside, Scarlett reached out to them. It was as if she was talking to a child, thoughts so simple, but she told them to congregate behind her, and they trotted across, essentially blocking up the way for those coming after her. It would have been a much better blockade if there had been more time.

Then she panicked that the firebird was slipping behind. The bird had been flying here and there, usually unseen by Scarlett, but had succeeded in turning back or turning to dust many of her attackers. But Calandra was overwhelmed, and she had a feeling the firebird was on the verge of exhaustion as well.

Scarlett had been running for some ten minutes and already her body was exhausted. She had a sore neck from constantly looking upward, scanning for her route away from this place. But she kept looking, hoping to see some means of escape. Then she saw him, a little man waving at her and encouraging her forward. Surely she had seen him before…Rodriguez!

She felt the hot breath behind her, but was again startled as something gave out a cry. The cry ceased and she was clear again. Lifting her feet through the now heavy snow, her every limb screamed at her but the cries from behind made her drive on. Rodriguez was indicating to her to run and run hard. Scarlett never looked back even when she heard the cries of people falling to the ground.

Scarlett watched Rodriguez run past her, and she saw the scrambling bike, lying on the ground up ahead. There were spikes in the tires. She picked it up and sat astride it, trying to figure out how to activate it. Never having ridden a bike in her life, the controls seemed somewhat strange. She knew there was a throttle somewhere, and you had to turn one of the handles. Was there a key? Scarlett began to fumble here and there, reaching around, looking at the few dials and gauges. There was a speedometer, but that wasn't helping. She flicked the switch and some lights came on. That was it, nothing else was coming on or starting up. She turned her head to the sound of someone running up to the motorbike. It was Rodriguez, and his work of the last minute was showing, numerous bodies lying on the ground groaning, some motionless.

On reaching the motorbike, he jumped straight on between her and the handlebars but rather than sitting down, he stood up. He kicked a lever at the bottom of the motorbike and it exploded into life. Scarlett was grateful to hear the engine, and they began to roar away. Rodriguez dropped onto the front piece of the seat, pushing Scarlett onto the rear half. He grabbed the handlebars, and yelled at Scarlett to hold on. Previously she would wrap her arms around Calandra, but Rodriguez was smaller and she had to hold onto his shoulders in a desperate fashion. The bike bounced along as Rodriguez headed up into the deeper snow that was beginning to thicken around them. They seemed to be on some sort of path as the snow didn't compact underneath them.

"Calandra? Rodriguez, what about Calandra?" said Scarlett.

A simple shake of the head was the cold reply.

We can't just go. We can't just leave her! Something inside felt wrong about losing the woman who had rescued her so many times before. But below, the mountainside was awash with men. *Rodriguez is probably right as harsh and cold as it sounded.* But the firebird had disappeared. *Flame? Where are you, Flame? Had she succumbed too?* wondered Scarlett.

There was no fireball racing around. Then she felt a weight on her shoulder and the motorbike wobbled slightly causing Rodriguez to swear. There was a slight pain in her shoulder as she felt the bird hang on tight. *Invisible but safe,* thought Scarlett.

The motorbike roared away up the mountain and Scarlett cast a last forlorn look down the mountain where she could no longer see Calandra, just a mass of men. *Goodbye, you saved my life again.*

12

Austerley

"What are you doing here?" asked Rodriguez. The robotic voice took Scarlett by surprise, as the man was a mute. But then she saw the small device he was tapping into.

They had brought the bike deep into a small cave far up in the mountains. Although they were inside, it was still cold and Scarlett was beginning to shiver. She wrapped her arms around herself but was aware that the stare from Rodriguez wasn't much warmer than she felt. *I could really do with a roaring fire to sit beside.* Flame appeared, burning intensely, but so suddenly that it caused Rodriguez to take up a defensive pose before moving to strike the bird. Holding up her hand and stepping between the burning bird and the small man, Scarlett said, "It's okay. She's just keeping me warm."

"I can ask about the bird later, but why are you here? I sent for help, and they brought you into the middle of this?"

"Wilson got your call, he got your distress. The company sent Calandra."

"Calandra, yes, but why you?"

"After all of the attacks I'm wondering why too, believe me. We were at the zoo, the one at the top of Scotland, when the call came in. We took a submarine across to Europe but got attacked several times on the way. They seem to know where we are."

"She shouldn't have brought you. All I needed was a little help getting to the box again. The village was getting too hot for me to walk freely. Did you find it?"

"Find what?" asked Scarlett, "Do you mean the box?"

"The box I saw, but it had some sort of parchment in it. I never quite saw the words but it seemed important. They intend to take it and use it, but I don't know what it is."

"Calandra saw your mark on the building, that's why we went in there. We found the box, and we found the parchment. Calandra put it in her pocket. And now she's..."

"Don't go there, she's hardier than you think."

"I think she's very hardy," spat Scarlett, "but did you see the number of those things coming?"

"That's not a problem we can do anything about. Wilson sent me here because he heard rumours of strange goings on. It wasn't difficult to spot the creatures with their weird heads, and whenever they had secret meetings, the parchment was brought out. The discussion seemed to centre on a demon from what I could gather, but I don't know which one though. But it seemed they would use the parchment soon. I was going to get it myself, having tracked it to where they kept it. The trouble was, that with my investigations, I had become known by them. So I needed someone else to fetch it, but I couldn't give normal communications as I was being watched the whole time. Everyone remembers the big man and everybody remembers the small man, but normally they don't remember someone in the middle. I had hoped he'd have sent one of our quiet field workers. But Wilson sends the Ice Maiden and a buxom blonde."

In better times I'd have owned that comment, she thought. "He thought you were in trouble. But we need to get Calandra then? We need to go back and get her."

"You're going nowhere. What can we do if we go back? There's too many of them. It was like you said. They seem to find you, so we need to be on the move, out of the way before something worse happens to you. Besides where do they have her now, if she's alive."

I thought she was probably dead. But they could have her, a woman like her being held. And all for a piece of paper. They'll search her and find it. Then who knows what they'll do with her or to her? All for a piece of paper.

The thing with the markings? The voice came into her head. *Folded up. In the cold lady's pocket.*

It took a moment to realise this was Flame speaking. She was so close to her, but the bird was burning and Scarlett couldn't get closer.

You sent me back to the lady, when those creatures attacked you. The creatures I burned. I tried to get close to burn them away from her, but she waved her stick at me. There was paper on the end and she kept waving it at me. So I took it, but it wasn't food. I kept it in my mouth.

But it will be burned up.

No, it was in my mouth. I don't burn my food.

The firebird lost its flame and then flew gently to set down on Scarlett's shoulder. It began to regurgitate and gradually spat out a piece of parchment. Scarlett picked up the moist, sticky paper.

"That's it," said Rodriguez, "How did it get it?"

"Calandra gave it to her. She just told me."

"She told you, so this necklace, it obviously works with you?"

"Well, I can talk very well to her. She came from the zoo with me. And I've been able to talk to certain other creatures but sometimes it's hard. Not all are pleasant. But we should be thinking about getting Calandra. We need to go get her."

"No! Absolutely not. We need to get you to Austerley. We need that piece of parchment in his hands, so we can translate it. As Calandra didn't seem to think it's safe to leave you anywhere, I'll need to take you with me. Make sure you bring the bird, it's quite handy in a fight."

"Not sure I can get rid of her anyway," said Scarlett, "Keeps appearing on my shoulder." Then a thought struck Scarlett. "Did you say, Austerley?"

"Yes, Austerley. Why?"

"That's what Calandra said. She said to get Austerley's location."

"You spoke to Austerley?"

"Yes. Gave some mumbo-jumbo which is quite hard to remember. Something about some place and time, something that like, I don't know."

"Every word," said an earnest Rodriguez, "I need every word just as he said it."

Scarlett sat trying to ponder what she had heard on the phone but it wasn't easy recollecting. She sat going over it time and time again until at last she thought she had it. "Nebulos categorical exposition of Kazern. That's the book you want. That and Schroder's phantasmal extrodinare."

"Really, that's all he said? He really has a fondness for libraries." The small man became immersed in his device and began to focus the screen. Occasionally he would curse and shake his head. Eventually a smile came across his face.

"Yes, it's a library, but it's gonna be about a day's travel from here. We need to get going because he might be there for two days at the most. Given Austerley stated that over a few hours ago, time is ticking. You might not enjoy the ride stuck on the back of the bike, but I can't leave you hanging around."

Scarlett still wanted to go back and see what had become of Calandra but what else could she do? Rodriguez was insistent that this parchment meant so much more. She also got the feeling that he wasn't telling her everything. Maybe he had suspicions he didn't want to bring to light at the moment. And they were being tracked. *Maybe that's why Rodriguez wants to get on the move again. Nothing to do but saddle up and go find this Austerley man. Maybe Rodriguez can get in touch with Wilson then and get a rescue organised for Calandra.*

Reason said this was the correct option, but Scarlett was finding that truth to be uncomfortable as they continued across the mountains, occasionally coming back down where they were unable to pass along the top due to snow. Weather conditions made finding paths high up the mountains awkward. Often there were no roads, just poor scrambling tracks, but Rodriguez seemed to know where he was going, causing Scarlett to just sit and keep quiet on the back of the bike.

Everything was snow-covered with green valleys below, and they never reached the valleys as the small man wanted to keep high. Amongst the snow, he admitted you can see everything, but then he could see them coming from further away. Scarlett had no idea what he was going on about but he was the expert, she was a novice, so she trusted him. She had hung on with her arms around his shoulders until she had fallen off once when she nodded off. Taking the chance for a break himself, Rodriguez said he would fetch some water.

There seemed to be a small pond in front of them but it was frozen over, seemingly solid. Rodriguez smashed his elbow into it time and again and Scarlett watched slight cracks form until the ice broke inward and, the little man could reach down with a hand and scoop some water up from below the surface. Waving Scarlett over, he let her sip from his hand. The water was so cold but clear and welcome.

"Mr. Austerley's up the slope," said Rodriguez via his small device.

Scarlett looked up into a snowy blizzard that seemed to cover the higher regions of the mountain. "You said he was going to be in a library. Who puts a library up there?"

"You understand the places that Austerley knows are not normal places. He's not a frequent visitor to your local library, but anyway, it's not that strange for Austerley to be here. Listen carefully. When you go up, you are going to decide whether to give the parchment at the meeting by what's outside. If you're inside, he'll be safe because another protector will be watching him.

"You won't miss Austerley, he's very easy to recognise. He's well over 6 foot, he's got hair that looks like he's forgot what scissors were for, and he's also got a prosthetic leg. If you're in any doubt, give him a good hard kick." Scarlett nodded. "And another thing, just be careful what you say to him. He's liable to go half-cocked about this, but you need to take in everything he says. You need to tell me what he says once you come back out. Understand me?" Scarlett nodded. "Good, time to get going."

They got back on the bike and headed up into the mountain.

It was tough going with the snow falling all around but Rodriguez seemed to pick his way through the mountainside. It wasn't long before she saw a shadowy building emerging from the blizzard almost unseen on the mountainside. As he drew closer, Rodriguez pointed to the door in the side. Once off the bike, Rodriguez indicated Scarlett should go and knock on the door. Wrapping her arms around herself to keep warm, she trudged along, fighting the blizzard towards the door.

On reaching, she thought about knocking but if nobody answered, she'd still be standing in the snow. So she tried the handle. Her hand was shaking with nerves as she twisted the handle but then she felt a comforting weight on her shoulder. Scarlett smiled. It was handy having a protector right beside you. With the door opened, the wind howled through, and she quickly shut the door behind her. The snow on her feet started to melt when they touched the stone floor, and she realised that there must be some heating in the library. The air, while not overly warm, wasn't as cold as outside.

There were bookshelves everywhere stacked with seemingly antique books. There were a few shelves that seemed to be in a state of decay and there was a mustiness to the whole place. It also had three distinct levels. Scarlett was on the bottom one and ahead of her were some stone steps that led up and up. She could see the stone staircase wind up to the highest level.

Cautiously, she walked forward, looking down the aisles of books on either side. There was no one, so she walked up the stone steps to the middle level. Here the lines of books were not so obvious. The shelves seemed to weave around in a semi-circular fashion. From the central aisle she couldn't look down the length of them at all. So she turned and walked down each aisle in turn.

As she rounded one of the corners, she came face-to-face with something. It was humanoid in shape, but its left hand didn't have a hand at the end, more like a couple of pincers. Its face was showing a smile—at least what seemed to be a smile—and the eyes were glassy and yellow. It looked happy, almost delighted and very interested in her.

Her heart pounded. She wondered what to do before from the depths of the figure came a quiet "excuse me". The creature stepped to one side, and she saw it wore a grey garment. Scarlett sped on, not wanting to see what was underneath.

She rounded another corner and ran right into a man. He was heavily tattooed and wore no smile. She stepped aside to let him through and began to wonder just where this Austerley was. She returned to the centre of the middle level and noticed that there were tables at the far corner. At these wooden tables, each with a classic bench, she saw several types of people. "People" was a conceit as really most of them were not people. Also, not one of them fitted the description Rodriguez had given her of Austerley. She focused on the task in hand as she watched one of the tables occupants use four hands on a book. *He's not here. Time to go up. And quick!*

Scarlett walked up the twisting staircase to the highest level and noticed the books here were all invariably falling apart, held together by extra bindings. There was some detail at the end of each aisle that indicated whatever books they were, but the language was nothing that Scarlett recognised. At the top of the staircase she saw what she thought was her goal. A man stood with a book in his hand, turned away from her. He had broad shoulders with a khaki jacket on and combat leggings. There were thick boots as well, but what really convinced her it could be Austerley, was the scraggly hair. From behind he didn't look in shape, a hulk of a man. Scarlett was going to open the conversation but she remembered what Rodriguez had said and she calmly walked up behind the man, and gave his left leg a good hard kick.

"What the hell?" The hulk of a man hopped onto one foot. "What are you doing?" he said.

"Oh, sorry," said Scarlett, retreating slightly from the now angry man.

"Just what are you are looking for," said the man. "And what the hell was that for?"

"Are you Austerley? I was told you've got a prosthetic leg. He said you had a prosthetic leg."

"The woman on the phone, Calandra's friend." The man rolled his eyes as if Scarlett was a complete simpleton. "Yes, I am him. But it's the other bloody leg, woman. Bloody clueless these days."

"Watch your mouth! What the hell are we doing up here anyway? Back end of nowhere."

"It's not that easy to find," said Austerley. "Why do you want me?" asked Austerley, "Damned inconvenient."

"We've got this parchment. Calandra said you would know what to do with it," said Scarlett. "Never mentioned you would be a grumpy old arse."

Austerley shot a look of contempt in her direction. "Where is it then? Do I get a look at this parchment?"

Scarlett opened up her jacket and pulled her top forward to reach inside for the parchment. She was careful how she manoeuvred her top but became acutely aware of Austerley staring at what she presumed to be her chest. "Do you mind? You never seen a woman before?"

"You're a stunning delight," said Austerley, "Would you look at that."

Scarlett was creeped out completely now. She closed her jacket quickly.

"No, no, no," said Austerley and reached forward to open the jacket again.

Scarlett kicked him again hard and not in the prosthetic leg. "Bloody pervert!" she said. "I'm taking that from no one."

"No," said Austerley fighting through the pain, keeping her jacket open. Scarlett tried to turn away, but she felt Austerley's strong arms grabbing her shoulders. He prized her arms apart and she saw him looking in a hungry, obsessive fashion.

"Just amazing," said Austerley, "just amazing."

Scarlett's hands were being held tight with only one of Austerley's almost to the point of pain while his other hand gently lowered her top to the point where her breastbone was completely exposed.

"Just amazing," said Austerley, "How long have you been wearing it?"

It dawned on Scarlett what was going on and once again she found herself relieved yet quite indignant that it wasn't her he was looking at, but rather just some necklace. She wasn't quite sure how that worked but anyway it was his fault. Then he cried out in pain as a small cut appeared on his nose.

It's okay, Flame. Stand down.

"And a bloody firebird too." Austerley laughed as he clutched his nose. "When Wilson said to me about the necklace, I thought he was joking. These matters are long gone, long, long gone. I was aware there were rumours there was once one in Austria, but where…no one knew. Because the real talk of these matters came from mad people. Initially, there were tales of dragons long, long ago, but these days so little is known about it. She used to use the necklaces all the time but some say she didn't need it. But it had sunk beneath the skin, you know how that is?"

Scarlett shook her head. "This is my first animal controlling necklace."

"It's nothing to be ashamed of," said Austerley. "Most of the people, I find, stay clear of anything this magnificent." He ran his hand along her breastbone and stopped very deliberately where the necklace was barely showing. Scarlett was aware the necklace wasn't glowing at the moment, in fact, if anything, it seemed to be more than normal.

"You see it? How did you know it was there?"

"I can feel these things," said Austerley. "You may not have heard that I fought a demon and returned him to his realm. Did Calandra not tell you about this? She didn't tell you about him either?"

"This is all wonderfully cryptic," said Scarlett, "But I came here for you to tell me what it says on that parchment, not have my chest admired."

Austerley never flinched at the comment. Instead, he continued to stare before slowly opening the parchment. He looked at it, studying carefully, but every now and again his eyes returned their focus on Scarlett. She noticed that each time, although he tried to countenance her face, his eyes were mainly on the necklace. He would glance up to her face, then back to the necklace. She couldn't help but think that he was studying her. He would mutter the word "magnificent" under his breath time and again.

"Well," said Scarlett. "Can you read that thing or not?"

"Yes, of course," said Austerley, "Just give me a minute." The first time he'd spoken, he'd been quite cold but now he was almost helpful. "I think we should sit down while I explain this to you," said Austerley, and he stepped forward, placing an arm around her shoulder. Taking her back to the steps, he sat down and indicated that she should sit beside him. He folded the parchment out onto his knee and began to point to some of the symbols on the paper.

"This is talking about creatures of the deep. Although the parchment originally comes from London, the words talk of a seafaring nation that no longer exists. It would have been off the coast of Finland, quite far up towards the Arctic. In their day, they travelled the world, but today the world knows nothing of them, their stories are held in places like this. You see, people don't know what's in the books, I mean the books not written in their time.

"The long and short of it is, this is calling for a worship of a creature of the sea. You would know it as a Kraken from contemporary folklore. People talk about the beast that would bring down a ship, but really, it was much worse than that. This creature courted civilisations on the coast, and indeed it destroyed many of them. Yet there are plenty who seemingly still tried to entice this creature. This parchment is a way of bringing it up from the depths. And then these civilisations would try to control it. Look, that word there, don't worry about the letters, that's a controller of creatures, a beast master. But as far as I can recall, no one's ever controlled a Kraken. If somebody has this parchment it would seem that they are trying to raise the Kraken again. And they came after you?"

Scarlett nodded.

"Then they want the necklace because they think it can control it. A beast master can't control it, but they must think that the necklace or a combination of both would do it. I don't know. The trouble with creatures, as opposed to demons or other gods, is that the brain implies that there is control, but understand, it doesn't always work like that. People bring them up, one from wherever, but ultimately, they can't put them back".

"A Kraken?" asked Scarlett, "You mean like the Kraken that takes a ship down to the seabed, Davy Jones and all that?"

"That's what the myth has turned into," said Austerley. "But this thing is much worse. The size of this creature compared to a wooden ship meant it probably destroyed the ship in an instant."

"So why would anybody want to bring it up?"

"These people, the ones chasing you, what do they look like?"

"Human," replied Scarlett, "Mainly human but their heads…"

"Are elliptical. They are trying something again. They sound like a runaway band of people I have met before. Humans giving themselves over to something else. These people would have worshipped the fish-god, Dagon, but this sounds like some splinter group obsessed with more than Dagon. Must be somebody or something at the core. Somebody has knowledge beyond what they would normally know."

"There is something else," said Scarlett, "Or someone else. Like a presence, at times it feels like it is on top of me. Moreover, it's like every man you don't want to be around you, too close, too personal, and it's right there controlling. Like a shadow sweeping over you."

"Can you physically touch it? Can it be struck?"

"Calandra struck it. Threw it off me, so yes, it can be struck."

Austerley stood and headed off into the piles of books on a nearby shelf. Scarlett watched him look up and down, sweeping along the line. When he got up, he had been awkward, his prosthetic leg forcing him into an unnatural action as he tried to rise. But he was buoyant as he limped off to the books.

He came back holding four different books, all of which were in a state of disrepair. Then he turned and took another book off the shelf closest to him, which looked almost new. Sitting down beside Scarlett, he beamed at her before flicking through the book in front of him. It was one of the old ones. After skimming through, he placed fingers in several pages, marking his place.

"Look." The book was open at a page showing a pencil drawing of a woman. She was stumpy, buxom with long blonde hair and a fiery look in her eye. She wore a necklace which seemed to be buried into her flesh. "Passarella, Constance Passarella. I'm not sure just how far back, but I think Constance is a relative of yours. An original beast master. You can see the resemblance. Delightful looking creature."

Scarlett stared. It was only a pencil drawing but it was uncanny. The hair, the necklace, the shape of her body. Inside, something tingled. As she continued to look at the drawing, she realised there was a slight indentation on the shoulder of the woman. Like some sort of weight was on it. Like a bird?

"A fire-bird probably," said Austerley.

"You can see it too?" asked Scarlett.

"Don't take this the wrong way, but there is an imperfection in your figure and there is one in hers. The dip on the shoulder is enforced by something. It goes against your natural curves."

"You can tell that from the drawing? I mean it's that obvious? I thought it was just me because, well, I kind of feel it there so I would look but…"

"You're dealing with something of an expert here, my dear. There are people who may run around who kick and punch and fight, useful in their way. But you're with the serious end of the business now. They have nothing on us." Austerley took the book to one side, and he opened up a new book. As he skimmed through the pages, it seemed to be a "Who's Who". Scarlett gasped as he put his finger in the middle of a page. "Look, recognise her?"

It was a woman in a breath-taking outfit that Scarlett imagined she would only wear in dreams with some very, very lucky man. But once she got over the initial shock of the outfit, she saw that long blonde hair and the short but curvy shape. And she saw the face, she saw herself. And around the woman's exposed breastbone there was a glow. "Is that me?" asked Scarlett.

"No, my dear that dates back 30 to 40 years ago. This book is like a list of people who have abilities, connections with things that go bump in the night, shall we say. And that woman had a true connection."

Scarlett watched his eyes roam from the book to the necklace and back to the book before looking up into her face. "That's the last of the beast masters. Glorious, stunning, powerful. A woman like you. She, I believe my dear, is your mother."

13

Ice Cold Fire

Calandra awoke with a start. Despite the lack of light, she realised that her arms were bound behind her by some sort of wire. She could feel the metal threads cutting into her wrists. They had removed her jacket, which was quite wise, for it contained a number of things in its interior, but she was still dressed in her boots, black leggings and black cropped top.

She felt the bruises from the fight throbbing on her face. In fact, her cheek felt like it was on fire which was a new feeling for her. It had been a while since she had fought that intensely and the strength of it had caught her somewhat by surprise. But she had been expecting them to attack when she realised that Rodriguez had left the mark. It was a mark made not with time and discretion but rather, one completed on the move.

The surroundings were damp, dank moisture was in the air and she heard the occasional lapping of water. As her eyes penetrated the darkness, she could see she was being watched by not one, but several men. Not quite men either, she thought, as their heads were off kilter and not quite right. Elliptical.

The things on the island were elliptical too. The island that she had no intentions of returning to even though it was now cleared of the strange inhabitants. Such a wild time when she first got involved with the boys, a time when she'd been forced into action and gotten herself involved with him. Although he was far away, he damn well appeared in every thought. Having started working for the organisation with him, she was now working for a separate part so that they would never come into contact.

Keeping this distance, she knew, was the right thing to do. But there were times when she wanted to go back, wanted the same closeness again and now she was stuck in this corner, trapped alone, and she wished he was nearby. *He came back for me, rejected the world and came for me.* Not that she hadn't saved him many times, but he had rejected his wife to save her. His wife had won in the end. His wife had won if you call losing your mind winning.

Calandra forced herself to stop thinking like this. With her mind reeling, she realised it came from fatigue and from a tiny bit of fear inside. When you've been through as many escapades as she had, you always wondered when the one was coming that you don't walk away from. Maybe this was it. At least she had gotten the parchment away from the horde, and hopefully the bird took it to Scarlett.

The girl's strange, thought Calandra, *not really cut out for this sort of thing. Then again, it had kind of been just dumped on her. From going from a girl who knew nothing about any of this to becoming a girl who was at the forefront must be something she was struggling to comprehend. Hopefully she'd gotten to Austerley. He could help.*

It wasn't that different from herself. Calandra remembered

when she had first gone through such a tragic time, finding the love of her life and then killing him. She remembered the shards of ice exploding over her, the storm around her. The cold, hideous laugh from the evil that was now part of her.

Some of the men approached and groggily she realised her legs were tied as well. They rolled her onto her front, shoved a pole between her legs and arms and started carrying her upside down. Loose hair fell over her face, and she watched the floor as she bobbled on her arms which screamed from the pain of being held. She tried to use her legs to carry more of the weight but the men at the rear were shorter than those at the front.

Looking at the rocks around her, she wondered if she was still in Switzerland. When the attack had come and she was surrounded, she had tried spinning her staff, had taken down so many of them, but they were relentless. She had eventually succumbed despite using her wings. Brutal and wild but to no avail as the sheer numbers had brought her down.

Where had they all come from? The houses? Too many of them, surely? On the island the elliptical heads came as the people transformed into frogmen, hideous creatures worshipping the fish god, Dagon. Dagon had tried to break into the world and then via another dimension. Twice Austerley had stopped him. And the last time, she had lost Kirkgordon.

The creatures, focus on the creatures. Elliptical heads but not transformed. Changed, yes. Not human, not any more. Well, not humanoid, they weren't really human to begin with.

Previously, they had been a group called the esoteric order of Dagon. E-O-D. But these elliptical headed people had no traits, other than the shape of their heads, from being EOD. There were no trappings of garb that resembled the decrepit fashion of the EOD. They also didn't seem to drink a lot. The previous creatures she encountered drunk like, well, a fish. Some on the island had even been fish heads, not frogs. *It's funny how these things seem to become normal. I guess I need to make some sort of plan if this old lady's going to make a millennium.*

Her party was rounding a corner when she realised she was now in another cave. In the middle of the cave was a fire, strong and bright, and she found herself being deposited on the floor, in a rough fashion, and then the pole was stripped away. Looking up at the roof of the cave, she saw a contraption comprising of runners and a large hook. There was a rope off the hook which allowed one of the creatures to drag it, so that it was over her position. She swore she could hear laughter as the hook was lowered in place between her hands. She then felt her shoulder blades screaming in pain as her arms were lifted into the air, dragging the rest of the body with it. Hanging, she was dragged along the runners and stopped over the fire.

Their hate was such that she could feel the force of it. At this time, it was a moderate fire, but the heat was strong enough to cause her to yelp. But then she began to feel better by turning to ice, fighting the heat, cold pushing it back.

A creature started shouting at the others. It was not a language that she recognised but it was clear what the intent was. A few creatures scuttled off to return with more wood, evidently for the fire beneath. Watching the fire increase another level she became colder. Calandra felt in control, driving away the heat. She was aware of the fact that her body was becoming fully ice, the leader of the creatures watching her closely. Fortunately, it wasn't a simple pair of leather trousers that she wore but they were in fact highly flame resistant as were her boots and top. This may have been puzzling to the creature but it was evident he wasn't about to stop. At this time, some creatures came back with liquid containers.

Calandra realised this flammable liquid would turn the heat up even more and she felt worried, she was coping so far but she needed to keep her cool. The creatures opened the containers that they brought back but instead of throwing them onto the fire, liquid was thrown at her. Her body was so cold she didn't even feel the liquid spilling on her and it dripping into the fire. With each drop, severe heat ripped up through her, and she realised that whatever this liquid was, it was producing a heat that she was not managing to push back. Little intense bursts of pain struck. Then the full amount of the liquid began to run off her and into the fire. The liquid ignited, and she felt the sheet of pain rollover. For the first time ever, she realised that she was beginning to melt.

Through the flames, she saw her boots and trousers were on fire and melting. She was melting too, but so were her bonds. At first she jerked and dropped very slightly. Then she fell straight into the cauldron beneath.

She heard a cackle. Not from the creatures, no, this was a voice she remembered. A voice she had only heard twice. Once when she lost Ferran and once when she faced Dagon for the last time. That time when he had saved her, and in return she had burnt his arms with the coldness, nearly killing him. The cackle was the witch she had faced all those years ago, the one who had cursed her. And it was laughing but not at her. The darkness was taking over; the rage was building. From thinking of her body melting, she began to hear the howl, to feel the bitterness, to feel like she was in the midst of a brutal snowstorm.

All of the creatures stared wide-eyed as the figure of an ice woman emerged from the fire. Around the creatures a wind picked up, which had no right to be there, deep underground. There was no time to move, no time to get away for they were being bombarded with cold and with ice. Calandra began to freeze, and she became see-through, like looking through the surface of a frozen lake to what was underneath. A laughter echoed round the chamber. The leader watched his fellow creatures turn to ice, and he saw them explode. The last thing he knew was the woman reaching up and blowing him a kiss. He shattered.

Calandra laughed, enjoying their destruction. Up until now, Calandra could turn the cold on and off at will, and she had learnt how to use it. After she had burnt Kirkgordon's arms she had trained hard, had fought to control it so if by any chance she could be with him, she wouldn't destroy him. But she now had to face it, she was never fully in control. But she fought hard against the witch that was inside, telling herself that it was over, that was done. She moved to the corner of the cave, hearing the wind slowing down, feeling her body change back to skin, back to flesh from the ice it had been.

It took a good ten minutes to fully feel she was back to normal, at least as normal as she ever was. But as she stood up, she realised she had lost her clothing in the fire. Not that she didn't have the self-confidence to move around. Wasn't as if these creatures were looking at her that way or even intended to do anything with her body. God help them if there were more and they did.

Starting down the passage that led from the cave, she continued in the opposite direction she been brought in. As she walked along, Calandra felt strange. She had always been happy with her body, always felt she had a figure to be proud of. Her upbringing in worlds far away from this one had made her unafraid to use it, to show herself in this state of undress. As she looked down, she realised the fire had taken a toll. Up from her belly, across part of her chest and touching up to her neck and her chin, she realised that her skin was no longer smooth. There were crumples and creases.

This must have been a burn, she thought. Her hand ran along the full length of the imperfection and she felt shame. Even though this darkness was within her at all times, with her looks she had always been able to create the fiction of being a perfect woman for any men around who took a fancy.

This will look wrong, like a freak. The freak I am.

She felt her black wings erupt from invisibility into life, and she wrapped them around, covering her body. This was a new feeling for her, and she didn't like it. She had wondered about people who had undergone plastic surgery to change their body, and she never understood because she had been so proud of her own. But now she began to understand. A tear formed in the well of her eye and crystallised. With a crunch from the flick of her eyelids, it fell to the floor.

Come on, she told herself, *I need to get out of here.*

The corridor seemed to be running uphill because it was a struggle to keep going. Maybe the fire had taken more of a toll on her than she imagined. She realised she was panting hard but kept going as she could see a light at the end, daylight. Waiting at the end of the corridor, she looked around outside for anyone. But no one came. She could spot no guards, no watchman left behind. Emerging into the snow-covered waste, the air was thin and her breathing continued to struggle.

Calandra found herself on a small plateau but turning around, she realised she was in the middle of a range of large mountains. *Am I still in the Alps? Could be.* The snow had fallen recently, and she could see no markings of any footprints or other types of movement of any creature. *If I was normal, then this would be very cold.* Looking around, she realised that the snow had fallen on something. There was tinge of grey under the snow, and she moved over to try and identify what it was.

Her wings fell behind Calandra as she bent down, moving the snow away from what was underneath. Underneath was a stone, grey and smoothed off and clearly planted in the ground. Widening her visual area, she saw a few darker patches and moved over to the next one again, applying the same process. Continuing this, she found ten stones of exactly the same colour and placed in a circle. She decided to remove the snow inside the circle and it took a few minutes to dig deep enough to find that something was underneath. There were lines defined by small stones laid side by side. Calandra worked hard to clear away the rest of the snow. After the work of at least an hour, she stepped back looking inside the circle.

There appeared to be several other circles crossed with lines running through them. It was nothing she had ever seen before. She wished she had a jacket so she could write this symbol down, but instead she stood and tried to commit it to memory. Maybe it was some sort of summoning circle. She had worked previously with different circles and she could draw some circles herself and move through portals to other worlds, but that was usually done in the dust. She doubted she could do it here in the snowy white rock. Besides, where would she go at the moment?

Calandra looked around to see if there was anything else

of note and wondered what to do. She could go back inside the cave, but she had come from the innermost part. There wasn't anywhere inside she hadn't seen. *Seems I've come from a dead-end.* This summoning circle was something but the markings were such that she needed to get back to Wilson, or preferably Austerley, to understand the detail. She hoped that Scarlett was with Austerley, at least he might provide some protection, a very different type of protection. He'd be amazed at her, especially when he realised what she could do. And if she found Austerley, she would probably also find him. He'd offer protection. It would be good to see him again. Her Churchy. *Kirkgordon, where in the world are you?*

This wasn't going anywhere, and Calandra decided that she needed to get down off the mountain. *Somewhere they must have a telephone*, she thought and so with her wings wrapped around, she began to descend. It took time to come down the mountain for everywhere there were treacherous large crags hiding drops and ravines but she was fortunate in that she had wings. Often, she just simply flew over them, gliding so she was able to bypass areas that involved dangerous situations. It didn't take her long to find the first signs of habitation. She headed directly for the lights of a large building outside of which were parked a number of snowmobiles. From inside, there was a hub of noise, and she realised quickly that it was some sort of drinking establishment.

On opening the doors, Calandra noticed the noise level drop slightly and several people looked to see who this newcomer was. As she walked into the bar, the noise level dropped significantly more, save for a few final murmurings and then total silence. Wrapped in her black wings, she made her way to the bar where a surprised young woman with wide open eyes suddenly let go a gasp.

"Anyone speak English?" asked Calandra. "Francais?"

"A little English," said the girl behind the bar.

"Excellent. I've run into a little trouble. Do you have a telephone I could use?"

The girl nodded and disappeared off briefly before returning with a small handset. Calandra let one wing slip away and reached out for the handset. There was a gasp from beside the bar. Realising that keeping the essentials covered with her wings was not that easy when she had to use her arms, she tried to reach out under a wing and preserve her dignity. Trembling slightly and hoping no one had seen the marks on her skin, she turned to them and said "Do you mind? This is a private call."

They stared at her for a moment before the woman behind the bar spoke in what Calandra thought was Romansh. The people turned away but some of the men glimpsed backwards. Calandra dialled the number and then the operator asked for a code. She spelt out the digits and letters, sixteen in total. The next part of the call was a confirmation of where she wanted to be routed to, but then a voice she recognised came online.

"Where are you?" It was Wilson, and he was concerned.

"Look," she said, "I don't know. Trace this number and come and get me. I'm getting some of the local men quite excited."

"What happened? All I heard was that there was a skirmish, and I haven't heard from anyone since."

"No one?" asked Calandra urgently, "I was hoping Scarlett got to Austerley. We found a parchment, something Rodriguez seemed to think was important, but we got interrupted. She got away up into the mountains."

"On her own?" asked Wilson, "She'd never survive on her

own."

"No, but she has company. The firebird went with her."

"So she definitely is a beast master? She definitely can control them?"

"Does more than control. They actually come willingly to follow her," said Calandra, "but I don't know where she is. And I haven't located bloody Rodriguez. I would try and contact Austerley."

"Last I heard, the boys were keeping a low profile as Ma'am was about to send them off elsewhere," said Wilson. "I'll find them. They haven't been in touch. I don't know if Scarlett's got hold of them, keeping it dark. Meanwhile, I'll get someone to you to pick you up. You said you were in a bar? What's your current status? Are you able to get to an airport, and I'll get to the tickets for pickup?"

"You're going to need to pick me up. Other than my wings, I ain't got a stitch on. I'll try and play it cool, but to be honest a single girl in the buff in the middle of nowhere is bound to be hit upon soon. I think the Swiss men are starting to look a little frisky. God help them if they make a move, Wilson, I'm not in the mood."

14

Findings in the Library

"Well, it's about time," said Calandra, "There's only so much a girl can do." She looked across at Wilson who had entered the bar. He was dressed as usual in his immaculate suit and simply walked across and reached out to her hand. She shook her head and nimbly stood up with her wings still covering her. Looking over her shoulder she said, "It's been a blast guys, but I'm afraid it's time I got some clothes on."

Together they walked out into yet more freshly fallen snow. Wilson led Calandra approximately half a mile away until they were well clear of this highest village and she saw the tiltrotor waiting in the snow. As they approached, the door opened, and Wilson, being the complete gentleman, assisted her into the plane.

"As keen as I am to find out all that happened," he said, "I will retire to the front of the craft while you dress and put your wings away." With that, he headed to the front of the tiltrotor as it took off, sending a blizzard of white to the outside world.

It was funny. Calandra had gotten used to her own style of

clothing and was grateful that Wilson had brought the same special clothing that she had taken to wearing. Her skin may have been cool, but she still felt the neat hugging of her boots and the feel of the leather on her thighs. The jacket once slipped around her shoulders made her feel whole again. With the echoes of the witch continuing to fade, she felt like she was once again in one piece. In recent times, she had reckoned she had a handle on the curse, that she was in control, but now she realised that pushed to the limit, the witch was still there deep within. Still, there was nothing for it. Scarlett was out there and needed help.

"Anything on Scarlett?" asked Calandra, as she walked to the front of the tiltrotor.

"Ah, good. You seem more like yourself again," said Wilson. "Been having some adventures." He raised his eyebrows and Calandra clocked his stare at the underside of her chin.

She raised her hand and touched the burn scar round her neck and from there imagined the rest of it across her chest and down across her waist. Austerley used to stare like Wilson was, years ago in Russia when they were close, but not like this. Not to the point of continuing while she was in discomfort. "It just scratched the surface."

"Such a large scratch. I think when we get back to base that will need to be examined. Our doctors, I am sure, will be able to assist."

Calandra shook her head, but she knew he was right. She didn't know if there was internal damage, but she felt fine. "Anything on Scarlett?" insisted Calandra.

"Well, actually, I was hoping you may have something," said Wilson, "After all, you did call me."

Calandra looked out of the window at the snow below. "She

can't be that far, I don't think I was out for more than a day. Not that I can be sure. There's no clues from the nearby surroundings?"

"It would appear that the village went back to normal very quickly. I passed on the way over, and I saw no signs of any disturbance. You mentioned you were on the phone to Mr. Austerley. By any chance would she have gotten to him?"

"I doubt it, not on her own. She's way out of her depth in this. Any mention of Rodriguez?"

Wilson shook his head. "Negative. No one has seen or heard of him, although to be fair, I haven't been involved in that search. Anything else from your time of capture?"

"There was a circle outside the entrance to the cave they kept me in. A circle of stones, apparently inside ten stones."

"Ten. Just confirm it was ten."

"Yes. Why?"

"Anything in the centre of that? Any pattern?" Wilson was becoming intrigued.

"There were a lot of crisscrossing lines."

"Can you draw it?"

"I can give it a go," said Calandra. Wilson's annoyed look sent her mind scurrying, desperately trying to rethink what the image looked like.

"More and more it seems we need Mr. Austerley. I had hoped to keep Scarlett and him apart. He has a fondness for the strange, as I remember his fondness for women who are strange too." Calandra raised her eyebrows at this. "Yes, my apologies, but with your abilities in my world you are a wonderful asset and also a well-rounded person but not in his world. You are a delight, a curiosity. Not merely an attractive woman who can do a job. You tugged the heart of

Mr. Austerley, he sees you as something special."

"I am special," said Calandra, "He always knew that." Her words came from a morose, external voice which surprised her. She knew she was missing Kirkgordon, and she knew he was tied to another. But she recalled her time with Austerley. Back in the day, he had picked her out as the stranger of the strange, wild and fun times as they roamed the darker side of the city. She enjoyed playing the vamp, enjoyed being the object of wonder. And to be fair, the last time he had nearly ended the world, he had thought he was her saviour.

"If Austerley was going to meet someone," asked Wilson, "Where do you think he would meet them? In the vicinity of Switzerland, obviously."

Calandra thought for a moment. Books, books, books and more books. One of the few places Austerley really knew inside out were libraries. And not the municipal ones, rather the ones with the books you don't normally see. The ones which had books people shouldn't see. They were usually out of the way. If he wants to meet someone, and he thinks he might need to impress them, then he'd go to one of his favourite haunts. If he's amongst the books, he'll feel comfortable because then if they ask questions, he'll be able to just roll over and grab a book from the shelf. He liked to do that in Russia. Heck, he wooed me in a Russian library.

"Okay, Wilson, if we take it that Scarlett has a couple of days on us, and she can do more than walk because of the firebird or someone else. And given we are here on the edge of Switzerland and given the terrain, let's be generous and say she can cover one hundred miles. I can think of a few places he might go. Although if it's a woman he's seeing, it'll be impressive, well in his eyes anyway. It's got to be Liv yo nan syel la. High in the Alps, full of some of the strangest creatures ever seen. We watched the sunrise on the top of it once. You misjudge the person he is. He really can be quite sweet."

"I will take your word for that Miss Calandra and take your judgement. Allinson," he said turning to the pilot, "you want to be heading for about here." His finger pointed on the digital map in front of the pilot, reaching into part of the Alps that looked barren.

The library was miles from anywhere, a rendezvous point that was clear of all onlookers. Allinson guided the tiltrotor close to the library in question, but due to a blizzard in progress, he had to land her somewhat down the slope where Wilson, in a rather tasteful overcoat and bowler hat, exited the aircraft followed by Calandra.

One of the items that Wilson had brought along was a spare staff. Calandra wasn't sure where her own was, as it had been stripped from her when she was in the cave, and she did point out that this one was inferior. The ones with which you can make fire at the end, the ones from Ferran's people, this was not. But then she remembered how she had gotten the staff and that brought back the time of the witch and his exploding into ice fragments.

Ferran, she thought, *dear Ferran, he wanted me by his side.*

With the recently fallen snow, there was no way to know if anyone had approached the library within the last hours, and Calandra wondered on the best approach and cover given that there were so very few spaces to hide in. Anyone on patrol as sentry around the library would no doubt see them. Calandra saw that Wilson allowed himself to be seen. He carried a gun in one pocket and a short blade in his jacket. It didn't sound like much but Calandra knew that, like his previous boss, Wilson was capable of handling himself.

Snow continued to fall as they approached the building whose outline they could just see through the blizzard. On a clear day, it must have been an impressive sight and she remembered the silence watching stars with Austerley. *Good times,* she thought, *they were good times.* It was then she heard the slight crunch in the snow. Wilson reacted to the sound by scanning, anticipating an attack. Calandra went to turn as well but instead she felt on her back the prick of something sharp, metal. And yet the intent was not to hurt but was more like a gentle tap to wake her up.

"I think we can hold it right there," said a voice she remembered. "I wasn't that sure if it was you. Still can't decide if your hair's better up or down."

Calandra turned slowly, worried her emotions would cause her to run, to cling to a man she couldn't have. It was a pain that she didn't want but that she knew so well.

"Ah, Mr. Kirkgordon, so Mr. Austerley *is* here. That's good to know at least. By any chance do you know if he's got a young woman with him?"

"Yes, he's inside, Wilson. So is the blonde woman. I think he's quite keen on her."

"Well, I think I'll head in and catch up with them. Any sign of being watched?" asked Wilson. A shake of the head from Kirkgordon, and Wilson continued, "Good, keep it that way. I'll leave you two for a moment, I'm sure there's plenty to discuss. When you're done, Miss Calandra, join me." Wilson trudged off through the snow to the door at the front of the building.

Calandra stared up into a face that was smiling back. The smile appeared genuine but weary. She drank in the view of his broad shoulders and stocky build. While not incredibly lean, he was always toned. Then she went back to his eyes. As much as every other part of him couldn't, his eyes always gave away just where he was at. She saw hunger, but she also saw his wife pulling him away. The love of his life that was now a basket case, a woman he couldn't have. In his eyes she saw herself.

"How's Alana?"

"Well, not good. Nightmares, harming herself. It's not good, even Austerley's baffled by it. And yet, he is the only one who seems to be able to get through to her. It's because he's been there. He looked at Dagon as well, but I guess when you're unhinged to begin with, it doesn't have the same effect."

"Now, now. You know, I do hope she gets better."

"I know," he said. His hand went forward and took hers. "Cold as ever. What's up?" he asked, "What happened? And what's the new scar?"

She unzipped her jacket open and pulled up her crop top without any sense of shame. Turning so he could see the scar at its fullest despite the obvious amount of flesh she was presenting, she watched him drink her whole in before he reached forward and grabbed her hands. Before Calandra could speak, he put a finger up to her lips. Calandra nodded. She looked at his arm, knowing the damage she caused underneath but there was something else about him now.

"It works very well," he said. "I can even get feeling out of it. Just amazing what they can do. There's another neat touch. Watch this." A small crossbow emerged from within his arm accompanied by a whirring mechanical sound.

"That's neat," she said, but she could feel her eyes beginning to well up. "I should go. I really should go." She went to walk past but he continued to stare intently. Without asking, he grabbed her, quickly forcing his lips to hers, and she responded. But just as the passion erupted they stepped back, as if there was someone nearby and their private bubble had been breached.

"Take care," she said, "Take really good care. Take care of him too." She turned her back and walked toward the entrance of the library. She knew he would be watching every last step of hers. She strutted like some fancy bird knowing it was being watched. *But this was all just show, just frustration. His heart was still with his wife. Well, that's what he'd always say.*

She opened the door and stepped inside the library. Immediately, she saw Wilson, Austerley and Scarlett at the highest level. Ignoring all around, she raced up the steps. Her heart was still beating fast from the outside encounter, and she looked somewhat flustered.

"So you've seen him?" said Austerley.

She nodded. "He's been hurt."

"He is not up for discussion at the moment. I think we should focus on where we are at, Mr. Austerley," interrupted Wilson. "Have you been making any progress? What's going on?"

Austerley was taken aback by Wilson's rudeness, and Calandra reached up to kiss Austerley on the cheek.

"Good to see you standing. Keep an eye on him."

Austerley was a little overcome but deflected by saying he needed to get a book to show more of what was going on. As he walked away, Scarlett took Calandra by the hand.

"You're alive. Thank God, you're alive. I didn't know what to do except for Rodriguez..."

"Rodriguez is okay?" asked Calandra.

"Yes, yes. He was up the hill above the house. He finally brought me here to meet Austerley. Austerley is quite something, he showed me my mum."

Calandra raised her eyebrows. "Your mum?"

"Yes, he's found my history, he's found the beast masters. He really is quite something. I guess you must know that."

"Yes, he's always been at least a friend. A very good friend. He once sacrificed the world for me."

"What happened?" asked Scarlett.

"He thought I was dead, so he decided to save the world instead."

Scarlett was somewhat baffled but then Austerley returned from the aisles, and Wilson insisted the conversation return back to operational matters.

"So, according to Mr. Austerley," said Wilson, "It would appear that this necklace is one used by the beast masters of old and has a strong controlling effect. But there is a possibility of something else. Miss O'Meara has talked about dealing with a shadow creature and that hints of something very old and very dark."

"But the something is the concern," said Austerley. "Scarlett said that she had this shadow man following her. Combined with the circles Calandra saw, I believe that the shadow man is a precursor. Once his actions are complete, or at least ready, the demon will come."

"What demon?" asked Calandra, "What are we really dealing with here?"

"Not sure," said Austerley, "But we're going to find out. I'm taking Churchy with me and we'll investigate these stones. Wilson says there was a circle of stones with other small stones apparent inside. Do you think you could draw it for me?"

Calandra nodded but inside she was worried she might not remember it. Austerley led her to a small table. Paper and pen were placed in front of her, and she began to sketch out from memory. It was not easy, and she reckoned she had about a quarter of the drawing done when Austerley snatched it away.

"No way, no damn way," cried Austerley, sending a few of the stranger locals in the library running for cover.

"Give me that back!" yelled Calandra.

Undeterred, Austerley slapped the paper back down on the table and began drawing in the rest of the design. Calandra was astounded.

"They're collecting the horde, they're collectors...the horde, don't you see?"

"The horde," asked Scarlett, "What do you mean, the horde?"

"They are assembling their army. To go to battle with his army and him when he comes... It would be hard enough if it was just him, but all these creatures too?"

"What creatures?" asked Wilson, "And who will be hard to beat?"

"Because this is an older demon, I don't know. I don't know its history, but this shadow creature, it will belong to an older demon. And these creatures it brings will be older creatures, and it's taking up from beneath the ground, from beneath time when this earth had creatures on it that it doesn't have now. Things from another time and from other worlds. This is the fifth of the sequence. They have dug up others already. They are looking for the fifth." Austerley grabbed the sheet of paper, and he began to start making calculations.

"Why bother with the necklace?" asked Wilson, "If they are just conjuring up these creatures, why the necklace?"

Austerley broke off his calculations looking indignant at the ridiculousness of the question. "Because with it, you have real control over them. He can then control and can take charge. She might be able to." A finger thrust out at Scarlett.

"Me? I thought the neck…"

"Thought what? It was all the necklace? No! It just amplifies what comes from within. It's within you!" cried Austerley.

"A bit more decorum please, Mr. Austerley," advised Wilson, "We may be alerting a few of the locals."

"Now," said Austerley, "You need to get to Edinburgh."

"Why?" asked Calandra.

"Because that's where they'll be. That's the next in the sequence. You need to get there and you need to get there quick. I don't know what they'll be bringing through, but you need to be there and you need to trap it. The less of these creatures he gets, the better it will be for us. Where's Churchy? Wilson, get Churchy. I need to go."

Wilson didn't hesitate and disappeared down the steps. Austerley turned first to Calandra and placed his hand upon her cheek. She began to go translucent, and Scarlett saw the wonder in his eyes as he looked at her. As the skin returned to pure white, she saw genuine affection. Austerley kissed Calandra on the cheek before she whispered goodbye. Turning around, he took Scarlett by the hand.

"Trust in yourself," he said. "She'll look after you and shall fight like nothing you've ever seen, but the real power lies with you and me. These things that come through, these things that you'll face, they are evil and they will mess you up, so you have to fight with everything. Do not hold back. Do not hesitate in using everything you've got. It's the only way to survive. And I hope you survive."

Scarlett was aware that he was looking all over, and she

was caught off guard when this large hulk of a man pulled her close and kissed her on the forehead. He then turned, shambling back down the stairs as the door to the front of the library opened. A figure stood there beside Wilson. The man waved, and Scarlett watched Calandra wave back. And Scarlett saw that she was gone, gone into a different world for a few moments. *That's him,* she thought, *that's him.* They then disappeared out the door, and the women were left together for a moment.

"Austerley really likes you," said Calandra, "I've never seen him stare at anyone like that."

"Really? He never stared at you like that?"

"Maybe back in Russia. A long time ago. Sorry girl, I'm afraid you're a freak like me."

15

Edinburgh

*E*dinburgh *at night is somewhat spectacular,* thought Scarlett. *It's a pity that we had to land some way away so as not to raise public worries.* There was no time for sightseeing as Scarlett and company raced through the streets towards the castle. The castle stood high on a hill in the centre of Edinburgh and was a glorious fortress of old, with its high walls blended into the sheer drops below.

However, there were roads that led up to it, some of them quite famous such as the Royal Mile and it was along this that they now travelled. There were shops and pubs along each side, but at 4 AM most were quiet, although in Edinburgh you were never quite sure when the pubs fully shut, if they did at all.

Scarlett had been here once on New Year's Eve when the place was absolutely full, "rammied" as a local said. She had danced the night away and spent a few indecent moments with a smooth talking man from Liverpool. She remembered that was one of her key moments in learning not to drink too much.

As they neared the final piece of road towards the castle, Scarlett realised that there was a temporary stadium built in front of it. It was closed off at the moment, but she could see the high, interlinked stands which formed the bowl around the approach to the castle. It was there for the annual military Tattoo, a time of drums and pipes and soldiers parading up and down this enclosed hub. Usually it was lights and lots of noise, mainly tuneful. But at this time of the night there was nothing, it was quiet and bolted up.

Calandra halted the party stepping into a doorway. Wilson followed. He wasn't in his dapper suit any more but in a black ensemble that was reminiscent of what Calandra wore all the time. Rodriguez had broken off from the walk to cover the other side of the castle. Scarlett suggested that he should go with them, that they should be partnering up, but Wilson advised that they could look after themselves and he was more concerned with keeping protection near her. There was a little bit of indignation from Scarlett before she realised he was probably right, beast master or not, she was hardly the fighting sort.

Her mind was still on the mysterious Mr. Austerley whom she had met in the library, and on the flight over she tried to pepper Calandra with questions about him. She found her responses moving to Kirkgordon, his partner. Then, in the middle of her sentences, Calandra would stop speaking, becoming lost in her own world.

She also wondered about her mum and she kept bringing, quite vividly, to mind the photograph Austerley had shown in the library. The woman had been older than herself, maybe late forties, but had the same frame, small in stature, wide shoulders, buxom like Scarlett and with long blonde hair that flowed out behind. She was definitely her mother's daughter, and she wondered if her mother was alone for most of her life. Or had she had many partners or a special one? She'd obviously been with someone at some point.

Calandra tapped her on the shoulder and pointed ahead. There were noises coming from inside the temporary stadium and Wilson moved silently away to the other side of the street. Calandra tapped Scarlett on the shoulder again, and she noted a man stepping out of one of the local pubs. His hat, which was wide brimmed, looked awkward on him, held at a jaunty angle as if it was about to fall off. He was walking unashamedly, glancing around him, and Scarlett was taken aback when Calandra stealthily walked up behind him and grabbed him by the neck, pulling him into the shadows. Scarlett was unsure what to do. She saw Wilson making his way into the shadows as well. Less than 30 seconds later, he returned to the far side of the street, and Calandra was approaching from in front.

"Elliptical head," said Calandra, "It's why they can't wear their hats properly."

"Where are these rings?" asked Scarlett, "Did Austerley give you a grid reference for the rings? He said he would."

"Grid reference?" He gave us some old-style coordinates that Wilson placed on the map. It's right underneath that temporary stadium. That doesn't seem right. People walk up and down this place every day. They should be on the ground in a circle, Austerley said, but I haven't heard anybody ever mention anything about stones on the ground."

"But would they?" asked Scarlett. "If they are really old maybe they're not evident above ground. Maybe they're under the ground, built over, unrecognised."

"We'll just have to assume they're there since we have no way of conducting any sort of topographical analysis to see. That sort of thing entails a lot of time, a lot of equipment and raises a lot of attention. We're hoping not to raise a lot of attention, in case you didn't get that. Wilson likes these things in the quiet."

"Where's Wilson anyway?" asked Scarlett.

Calandra placed an arm around Scarlett's shoulder and pointed ahead, high into the temporarily standing structure. There was a small shadow, almost imperceptible, and Scarlett realised it was moving.

"Wilson?"

"Oh yes," said Calandra, "You think I can move you, wait 'til you see this guy."

Keeping her eyes trained on Wilson, Scarlett watched him climb to the top of the seating and then move around in the darkness. Like any city, Edinburgh was never truly dark except for when the power was cut but there wasn't as much light high up, and there seemed to be little emanating from the stadium.

As she watched Wilson move along, she saw something in the distance beyond him move overhead that didn't look quite right. She went to grab Calandra's arm to advise her of this, but she was gone, moving quickly ahead. Scarlett wondered what to do and then ran after her. As she ran forward, she felt the ground begin to shake.

Up ahead, Calandra's wings exploded into life, and she jumped up onto the side of the temporary seating, high above Scarlett. Nearing the doors at the entrance to the seating, Scarlett realised they were locked, and more than that, she was exhausted. The road up to the castle was uphill and steep. She wasn't in the greatest of shape. However, Calandra was already up and on top of the stands. Scarlett heard a commotion. And a cry ripped into her mind.

It was like thousands of birds screeching at once. Dropping to her knees, she pushed back with her mind, trying to empty it of the sound but it was incessant, wild birds chattering all at once. Her hands were splayed out on the ground supporting her weight, but she was struggling to stay off the floor and looked like a worshipper at the gates of a temple.

Come on girl, get rid of this.

Slowly, she seemed able to push back and move the sound away. It was still there, it was still screeching, it was still one million birds in constant chatter, but it was also a cry for help. Though there were no distinct words, the meaning came through: *They're coming after us.* Big Bird, big threat. The ideas were simple, a feathered talon. She pushed herself back up, standing upright again, but then sought something with a mind. She found him on the other side of the street. *Get me up there, Flame.*

For those unaware of the firebird, they would have put Scarlett down as a sorceress. She seemed to take to the air without effort and gently land atop the standing. But Scarlett knew different, and she felt the downdraught from the wings above her. She was quite a weight for the firebird, but it never complained, and at least the trip was short.

As she set down on the top level of the seating she saw Wilson dispatching several people with elliptical heads. Calandra, however, was racing towards the centre of the stadium. The solid floor of what appeared to be tarmac had become a circle of molten black. Racing forward, Calandra dove her arms into the molten material as she became translucent. The molten circle began to freeze over slowly, a little bit at a time.

Down there! Scarlett felt her shoulders grabbed, and she was flown to the centre of the stadium. Dropping just outside the molten circle, she became aware of men running towards her. As the talons left her shoulder, the firebird became visible and started to burn. She didn't look, but she heard cries of pain behind her and felt the heat. There were no feelings of remorse from her, after all, these were the bad guys, and what was happening in front of her was far more worrying.

Initially, the ice from Calandra had made its way over half of the circle. But now the ice was melting. Returning to its molten nature, the circle was beginning to flow. Calandra herself was becoming less translucent, returning to a pale white skin, but her hands were still immersed in the molten liquid. Then slowly, Scarlett watched Calandra's arms begin to redden. The jacket she had been wearing was burning away, leaving what should have been pure white arms. But they were red and getting redder by the second.

"Get out!" yelled Scarlett, but Calandra seemed to be in a world of her own. And then she screamed.

Scarlett ran around the edge of the molten circle, desperately grabbing Calandra's shoulders. She pulled hard but nothing was moving. *I'm so weak dammit.* She'd never been a person for the fitness class, she had never pumped weights, and now she was desperately regretting it.

She looked for Wilson. He was occupied, seemingly swarmed over by lots of men. She shouted out for Rodriguez, but there was no answer. Calandra was now yelling in agony. Scarlett was feeling the heat from her, something that never had happened. She'd always been cold, cold to touch but now she was positively warm. She had to pull away and get clear. Scarlett couldn't help. But she was never alone, for she was a beast master.

She didn't have to form any words when it happened. It was like a connection that didn't require speech, almost as if she was one with him. Scarlett fell away to the side as the firebird grabbed Calandra by the shoulders, pulling her from the molten material. It set her down and then stood close as some of the strange men moved in to attack. The bird burned, and the men began to flee.

Thank goodness, thought Scarlett and turned her attention back to the circle. It was now bubbling, the heat emanating from it was intense. She saw molten rock, emerging so hot, she thought that it might kill her if she came in contact with it. She ran clear. Just a few seconds later, there was a loud explosion and molten rock leapt into the air. The eruption of this dangerous liquid rock was short lived, and Scarlett turned back to see a hole in the ground. At first she wondered what was in there. Then her mind became swamped by something else.

She remembered her school, being bullied by the girls who used to pick on her constantly because she was different. Picked on because womanhood reached her before the others. Then picked on because puppy fat had come with her growth. And then because she didn't have style.

The taunting had always been done by girls. They had been wicked, heartless, giving constant abuse. And now those voices returned. It was like a pressure wave, but a wave that was still increasing. There were no specific words, just unspoken accusations, and she wondered what was coming out of that hole.

And then came a cackling like witches, but much shriller, like a maniacal bird song that had been ground and ripped apart and put back together. There was a beat of wings and creatures raced out of the hole. One made a beeline straight for Scarlett and landed in front of her. Scarlett saw soft feathered wings emerging from the body of what appeared to be a woman. The hips were there, but there was none of the beauty. Instead of feet there were clawed talons. There was a woman's face, but it possessed a more pointed and jutting chin, and instead of hair, there were feathers rising from behind the head. There was nothing beautiful about this creature, the woman's body underneath was mangled in a horrific concoction of bird and human. Scarlett recognised it from the books of mythology she'd read. She saw the tormentors, those who had persecuted working Phineas.

You're pathetic, you're weak. A lack of beauty, a lack of strength, a child of a woman. You'll be crushed.

The words rang out, telling her that she was no good for anything. But this time it was a true voice, for the creature in front of her was speaking out loud.

Scarlett pushed back. *Get back in the pit you came from, go!*

Then came the reply. *You think you can control us, beast master? You think that necklace gives you control over me? You fraud, you don't deserve to wear it, you control nothing.*

Afterwards, Scarlett presumed she had been struck by a wing because she never saw it arrive, all she knew was the next moment she had been flung across the stadia floor and clattered into a sign at the bottom of the seating. Her head was ringing from the collision, and her shoulders were aching as she saw the foot of a harpy, its sharp talon reaching for her head. But then came the fire. The harpy gave out an unholy screech as it took to the air followed closely by the firebird.

With her groggy eyes, Scarlett counted at least six harpies

with the firebird at the centre of them, whirling around. Calandra was still on the ground, the heat leaving her arms, but she lay motionless. There were several of the strange men around, but they were being occupied by a small man. Scarlett felt a little hope inside seeing Rodriguez had joined the fight, and she began to sink back towards the ground, exhausted and in pain.

Something cradled her neck and then pulled her up. "No time for that Miss, we need to fight and you need to get hold of those things up there." Wilson's face was suddenly before her.

"But," she muttered, "They don't listen, they don't listen."

"You're a beast master, you have the power."

"But I don't! They don't listen. Just in my head, just shouting at me, always at me, flooding my mind."

"Your firebird is getting killed up there," said Wilson. "You need to react. Flood their mind. Don't try and control them. Just make them do something they don't want to do. Get inside their head!"

Pulling Scarlett to her groggy feet, he punched past her with his left, a hard punch to someone's head who fell to the ground. There was a little grin and Wilson turned and started engaging several other men who had started racing towards Scarlett. The battle on the ground was being held by Rodriguez and Wilson, giving cover to the women who had taken the initial blows. But up above, six harpies were ripping into the firebird and Scarlett could see the damage. Bits of flesh torn from the firebird came away as tiny burning flames before extinguishing and dropping as solid pieces to the ground.

"No!" she cried, "you won't have her!"

She sought the mind that was the weakest. It was the harpy

who seemed to be following the rest, the one who was never at the front of the pack. Like being at school where she was picked on, always the one of the back agreeing but never really instigating. And she went for its mind.

The creature pushed back hard and Scarlett's head was still ringing. Another piece of fire turned to flesh and hit the ground. Scarlett was desperate. She could see a glow emerging from her chest, the necklace taking on a life of its own, and she channelled her mind through it. The harpy succumbed and Scarlett could see herself rising, could feel the wings beating, the swish of the wind as she swept around. And she could feel the talons.

Without hesitating, she struck one of the other harpies across the face with a talon. The other claw, she swung out and cut across the neck of the creature who screeched before tumbling to the ground. Its wings flapped in a useless attempt to maintain height. There was a blow to her back, and Scarlett realised that the other harpies realised that their sister was now a threat.

But Scarlett attacked. With help from the firebird, she knocked a harpy off balance before a blur of fire scorched it, sending it tumbling to the ground. Scarlett grabbed a third harpy by the neck and then dove to the ground, pinning it, before breaking its neck. She felt the mind of the other three harpies moving, escaping. Wilson's voice could be heard shouting to contain them, but there was no containing these creatures as they flew off at speed into the night.

Scarlett then climbed her harpy up to the sky before diving back to the ground. Faster and faster she raced, the earth fast approaching. Just before she hit the ground, she dropped out of the mind of the creature. There was a sickening crunch and a break of a neck. Scarlett opened her eyes and saw the dead creature across from her.

Scarlett sat down, exhausted. Her mind was still reeling from having had so much evil within it but part of her knew she had succeeded. She'd become a beast master.

Then the firebird alighted, its white feathers in a miserable, unkempt state as it limped towards Scarlett. Large lumps of feathers were missing, deep gouges replacing them.

"No! Flame!" she gasped, taking the bird into her arms. The bird snuggled into her and let out a pained whimper. Scarlett let out her own whimper, thinking of all that she had done for her, saved her a dozen times and nearly sacrificed herself just to buy her time for escape. "Please don't die, Flame," she said between broken sobs. "Please don't die!"

Concern for the others pulled her out of the moment, and she looked around. Calandra was lying on the ground, motionless and forearms black. Rodriguez was over her, cradling her head and then he was shouting something at Wilson but Wilson was racing towards Scarlett.

"Get up, get up. We need to go," said Wilson, "We need to get out of here before anything else arrives. We need to get Miss Calandra out of here. I've never seen her burnt. I have never even seen her reach room temperature."

Scarlett surveyed the field of her first battle, her first rebuttal in which she'd been a participant and not just a victim on the run. Part of her was excited by the wins she'd earned this night. But as she looked at the victims around her, realisation dawned in her mind.

This was merely the creatures that had been brought forward, this was merely the side show. What if the shadow man came next time or, more importantly, if the demon had been raised? And, almost involuntarily, she thought of Austerley. Would he be facing it? Then she looked over and saw Calandra lying motionless, her arms black. Wilson had said "get up" but the emotions rolled inside. There was a gripping fear, a terror that she had killed creatures. Then came the anguish of seeing friends hurt, injured and—who knew?—maybe dead. She grabbed Wilson by the shoulder and burst into an uncontrollable rage of tears. She barely heard him say, "Later, now we go."

16

The Arrival

"We need to follow the harpies. The harpies are the thing. I know you don't want to hear this, you want to be somewhere else, but we need to follow the harpies."

Scarlett felt Wilson take her by the arm, dragging her along the street until he hailed a taxi. Taking up the rear middle seat, she was beside Calandra with Rodriguez on her other side. Wilson jumped into the front and immediately told the driver to step on it and take them to the edge of Edinburgh. As the taxi sped through the city, they skipped past neon windows and small shops and pubs, but Scarlett saw none of this.

She had driven a creature to its death. Calandra's arms were still black. That woman had never been hurt at all. At times Calandra had been under pressure, at times changed into something unique, something strange, but never had she been injured.

Scarlett was moping in the taxi until Wilson called everyone out. As it sped off, she wondered why she was standing on the edge of a football field, the bright moon lighting up the night sky but the night air now giving a chill. Calandra was huddled, obviously distressed by what had happened, and Rodriguez was paying careful attention to her. Wilson, on the other hand, strolled off onto the football pitch and then gently tapped the air. There was a sound of hollow tin and a tapped reply come back. Scarlett couldn't believe her eyes as one of the tilt rotors appeared.

"Get on board! We're behind, but if we're quick, we might just be able to track them."

"Track what?" asked Scarlett.

"The harpies, I keep telling you, the harpies. These are the first creatures whose arrival we've been at and these harpies, they will go somewhere, and they will go to a master. You don't just get brought into this world to suddenly sit around and do what you want. They've been brought here by someone who now owns them, who is in charge of them. A master for them, and we can find that person."

Scarlett dragged herself onto the tiltrotor and sat down on the seat. Without even thinking, she attached a seatbelt. It was all she could do to not stare at Calandra's arms. Jet black. Her face had returned to its pale colour, but she was obviously in discomfort. In fact, Scarlett wasn't sure she was actually conscious as Calandra wasn't moving but there was pain rolling across her face in waves. After a few minutes, Wilson reappeared from the front cockpit and sat down beside Scarlett.

"She's taken quite a hit," said Wilson. "I'll have to be a wingman for the next wee while. I'm not sure Rodriguez can handle looking after you, and besides, not knowing each other and how to work well together. You need talked through things, and he doesn't say much being a mute." Scarlett merely nodded, but there was little comprehension inside.

"When you say, wingman, for what?" asked Scarlett, "Where are we going?"

Wilson sighed. "I really do not know ma'am. I really do not know. I know we will trail these harpies, assess what is there and make a play. What play we invoke will depend on the situation. Realistically, I would rather not re-enter a fight because, quite frankly my dear, my best fighter is down, and I don't know what we will encounter with a novice on board."

"Thanks for that," said Scarlett, "Feeling better already. Confidence boosted."

"You need to understand, as much as I would like to keep you out of this, my prime priority here is to find out what is coming to this world and what to do about it. Those harpies are the only tangible thing I've got at the moment. Austerley may come up with some other form of horror to chase, but frankly, at the moment he hasn't given me anything but the Edinburgh circle and now these harpies to chase. So I need you to focus. Stop staring at Miss Calandra's arms and get your mind on what could be coming up ahead. You are here because you are of use. Be useful!"

As the man in charge stepped away, Scarlett felt very hollow. She remembered the days of wanting to be different, to be anything but ordinary. Right now those days felt a long way away. She'd been round a good part of Europe now, been underwater. She had been hunted by men with weird heads, but she'd also seen a woman who had become a friend go through extreme pain. And she killed something. Something real, something large.

She knew animals were animals, and she'd killed wasps and cockroaches before. But this was too much. Her mind replayed driving the creature into the ground, pulling out just in time. It was all her own work, all the destruction was hers. Overwhelmed by these thoughts, it took a while to realise that Wilson was speaking.

"The time's coming, and I need you to stand before these things again. We've tracked them to a castle. A ruin from the 12th century but something is going on inside. A heat scan is showing a number of, well, we think people. There's also things overhead. I am not sure how close we can get the tiltrotor but one senses a race against time. Sound analysis is picking up chanting, and it does not seem to be of a benign nature. I have patched it through to Mr. Austerley who is listening, but he is struggling with the language. He is wittering on about it being on his 45th language and the original text was not complete. But we will land soon enough, and when we do, we are going to move out. Are you ready Miss O'Meara?"

Scarlett stared straight ahead, unsure she'd even heard his words properly.

"Are you ready, Miss O'Meara?"

Scarlett looked up into his eyes and saw pain and uncertainty behind a determined mask.

"I believe we do not have a choice," said Wilson, "You have to be ready. There is no time to not be ready."

He disappeared into the cockpit, but he left the door open, and she could see his face. Normally it was dispassionate, giving away so very little, but now he looked worried and a little panicked. Placing his headset on, he began talking to someone. After a few questions and pauses when he was clearly listening to the answers being provided by the other end of his conversation, Wilson placed his headset to one side and marched back down into the body of the tiltrotor.

"They're bringing it up. Damn well bringing it up. I need Austerley. I need Austerley here now, and he's on the other side of the damn world. It's you, me and Rodriguez. I'm summoning everybody else I can, but they cannot get here in time. Austerley says they're bringing it up."

"Who are?" asked Scarlett, "Who the hell is bringing what up? What are you on about, man?"

"The demon, Austerley says they are bringing it up. Nothing simple, nothing that I've seen before, instead a demon of your ilk."

"My ilk? Am I demonic? Stop talking in riddles."

"It's a demon, and like a beast master, creatures will be drawn to it, but certainly not the ordinary kind. Every unholy creature will give themselves over to its will, and the demon will unleash these creatures on the world at different places and different times. In fact, maybe altogether! We need to stop it. We need to stop it from arriving."

Inside, Scarlett felt numb. Wilson and Calandra had seemed to deal with everything before, but in a night it had all changed. The harpies had caused such injury to them, and this demon was far worse.

Just exactly what is this demon? I thought demons were dealt with by higher powers. And one of her ilk, what did that mean? Scarlett put her hand down onto her breastbone and felt the necklace. *I was controlling the animals, controlling the harpies. Strong, powerful, but in the end, it just seemed hollow.* Another hand touched her shoulder, not with strength but delicately, as if it could almost hurt itself. As a familiar sensation sunk in, she recognized the cold touch of Calandra.

"I will be there with you," said Calandra. "I don't know

what's happened, I don't know how I was burnt, I don't burn. Cold, always cold, with which I burn other people. But listen to Wilson, stay close. Do what he says and just give them hell."

"It's easy for you to say that. Jumping here and there with your staff and ice, cutting that figure. Legs kicking out, arms swinging round all the time, a body that drops them before you do. You have it made."

"I was born in a cold place and ripped away from my parents when I was young. Raised in a completely different place, not just miles away, but a world away. So don't use me as a shield," spat Calandra. "This will be about you and what you can do. Don't let it control you, control it. There's something inside me that takes over, so now I've become something, destructive, black. Don't let that happen to you when the spark comes, when the surge of hunger and fire comes, don't let it be you that succumbs. Be yourself whenever you can, be yourself in this. It's a demon, and what they can do with their hands is nothing to what they can do with their minds."

"But I'm nothing like you!"

Scarlett felt Calandra pull at her shoulders, indicating that she should stand. She did so and found her jacket being removed to then be replaced by a different one. It was Calandra's, the black leather blanketing around her shoulders. It was a little tight, just under the arms but she didn't care, she knew she was getting the image. She knew what Calandra was doing and even when she went to zip it up and realised it wasn't going to connect one side with the other she didn't care. She may go into this looking inexperienced, but she'd look damn good in this jacket. Yeah this line of thinking was daft, stupid, but she felt like a femme fatale, just like Calandra.

Watching Calandra sit back down again, Scarlett saw her

look out the window and then drift off, becoming distant again. Wilson marched down the aircraft telling Scarlett to follow him to the back door of the tiltrotor. It opened up, and they were hovering just above the ground.

Three figures dropped to the ground, Rodriguez, Scarlett and Wilson. Wilson set off at pace across the ground that was white with snow and Rodriguez brought up the rear behind. Scarlett's legs were already screaming at the pace they were attempting. She could hear thick shouts in the air, clamouring words, whipped into the night that sounded evil with intent, even if the language was unintelligible. Wilson approached the side wall of the castle which was orange and glowing. Inside, Scarlett saw a creature she recognised atop the wall.

Without speaking, Wilson indicated he was going for a better look, but Scarlett grabbed his hand. "Don't!" she articulated. Reaching out with her mind, she could feel the harpy standing at the top. She pushed hard straight into its mind and felt it succumb almost immediately. The power was flowing through the necklace from her. She was getting better at channelling the device.

Scarlett focused hard to look through the harpy's eyes. She saw a figure beneath it which had an elliptical head and looked human. But it was wearing robes with strange markings on it whilst before it lay several creatures, presumably dead given the amount of blood. Gratuitous violence had been acted upon them.

The bile caught in her throat, but she continued to look around. There were a large number of men about, all with the strange heads and on the other side from them were a number of different creatures, most of which she didn't recognise. A couple of fires were burning, and the chanting was getting stronger and stronger. It reached a crescendo, and she could see the bodies in front of her begin to burn.

Something was coming up through the ground. Her eyes peered forward to see what it was, then a dark shadow struck across her mind and remained there.

He was here.

"Your mother was good at this, but she was mine in the end. You can't resist, for we are intertwined, you and me the way you want, I know. Such a beautiful creature born for subjugation—my subjugation. Give in to me, and I'll show you what you can really do with your power."

Scarlett fought to try and reach what was talking to her, but as she raised her head, she was abruptly thrown back from the harpy. She fell to the ground at Wilson's feet where he looked on anxiously. But then he turned, looking to the sky as a harpy flew down upon him. Despite meeting it with one hand and driving his limb deep into the flesh of the creature, its core took him up to the air. Scarlett from a prone position was then picked up by another harpy which Rodriguez slashed at with a knife. The creature would not be stopped and flew high into the air above the little man.

Scarlett tried to work out what was going on as she spun round and round above the ground. The creature dropped her a short distance above the ground, and she landed on hard, cold snow which soaked into her trousers. Almost immediately, she was picked up by some arms and dragged to one side where she was tied up to a wall, her arms either side held behind her and she hung forward. Wilson had been thrown to the ground close by, and she heard his cries as he was picked up and tossed about by the harpies. In her mind, she became angry, angry with herself for being grabbed. Then a familiar shadowy figure crossed her mind again but this time he was right in front of her face.

"Just lovely. I said you have your mother's neck and a fuller figure, but I don't think you have her skills. She was strong with the creatures. You control them somewhat, but she fought me a lot harder than you do. But now be in your happy, your natural state. Subjugated, happy to be mine."

Scarlett spat at the shadow but it flew outwards and down to the floor. This strange figure did not seem capable of holding anything. Wilson screamed again. Harpies were tossing him from one to the other, pecking at times. Scarlett looked over through the tears beginning to stream through her eyes. His body was racked first this way and then that. *That's enough. That's enough! You can't do that to him!*

As the anger built, Scarlett drove into the mind of one of the harpies. As soon as she had entered its mind she saw its sister directly across. A talon was lashed out into the face of the sibling and across the neck. Instantly the harpy fell to the ground. Scarlett turned her harpy around, looking for the next one. She felt the shadow again coming at her but she pushed back, channelling all her energy.

Like a tight fitting cloak, she wore the harpy's skin, commanding every part of the creature. Swooping and attacking crazily, she sent other creatures running as other harpies tried to reach out to it. Then she was pinned down. Thrashing hard, she forced a talon through the neck of another harpy. As it dispatched its sisters, Scarlett suddenly felt a hot pain and realised that the creature was being attacked with blades. She dropped back from its mind, letting it depart to its endless rest. From a hanging position, she saw Wilson still on the ground, evidently in pain but at least left alone for a moment.

"Good," said the deep voice, "You have a rage. You have a chance to become something more. You just have to let it go, that was your mother's undoing, she didn't stop short, and I had to kill her."

Scarlett had never known her mother, but this filth was claiming to have killed her. Driving hard with her mind, she tried to enter the creature's head. But there was blackness. A developing sense of despair. She was forced back.

"You don't do that with me. You can't comprehend my mind but you won't have to for much longer. Let your mind rest for the one much stronger comes now. Preserve your mind for him."

Scarlett opened her eyes and looked at the elliptical headed man in robes on the ground making a sign which seemed to display animals or something similar in the middle. Bending down, the man picked up what looked like a small creature. It was red, it was on fire. The man in the robes spoke with it and proceeded over towards Scarlett. Holding the little fiery creature in front of her eyes, she was mesmerised. She felt something inside, something dark and poignant. A mind being breached just like she was an animal.

She realised the creature was now inches from her as she could feel the heat from it, a white hot heat, almost searing. Opening her eyes, she saw that it was looking at her chest, where her breastbone was. A small red hand reached out and pulled down her top, ripping it so the breastbone was exposed. Scarlett watched in horror as the hand reached into her flesh. The pain drove through her body. Racked in agony and bouncing around, she felt something lever, something precious, something entwined was breaking away. Looking up through the pain, she saw the little creature was holding a necklace, her embedded necklace. Dropping her eyes back down to herself, she saw a line of charred flesh.

"I fear your colleagues are too driven for us to remain," said the deep voice. "I would bring you with us but at this time it is too much to get clear of, too much to set up, too many preparations. It has been good to see you again though you look a little shabbier now your weapon's gone. Still wild like your mother. She rid herself of me, took herself from me. That's why she ended up in the water. Some would say that was merciful, but understand she did what she did out of rage and that rage still sits on her daughter."

Scarlett felt the jarring blow to her jaw. She hung there in pain but too exhausted to speak.

"But we shall see if you are her child. I'm leaving a little something, something to feast on, or maybe it'll feast on you."

Scarlett was struggling to work out what was going on. Although groggy from the pain, she noticed the assembled collection of strange men and creatures disappearing and she also noticed a little man being pushed onto a crude frame. So Rodriguez had been caught too. It appeared that the whole team was down, and there was no cavalry coming to save them. But Wilson would have thought about this, surely. He would have someone coming soon. A special button to alert others. And then she heard the hiss.

Out of the corner of her eye she saw something slither along. At first it was just a flash, an indication of something different but as it slid into full view, she realised that this creature was massive. It had the head of the snake and a long body which ended beyond her sight. Four enormous fangs and a forked, flicking tongue. No doubt those fangs were carrying some sort of venom.

The creature slid over towards Wilson, wrapping itself around him and then dragging him with it as it then moved towards Rodriguez. The little man was pulled down from his position, enveloped by the coils of the snake. Scarlett was scared, terrified, and so weak that she struggled to move. What was she to do now? The necklace was gone, the weapon had been taken from her, taken by the little red fiery man, presumably a demon.

How long is this going to last before that thing rips us apart, sinks its fangs into me? But its useless. No necklace, no control. The one thing that made me useful. Without it I'm just a normal person. Nothing special.

But this is wrong. Heroes don't go down because they have dropped their weapon. They don't leave their friends in the lurch. This is life and death. This is it, so buck up girl. Mother fought him. He said that my mother had fought him. So come and get me. Come and get me now!

Scarlett could feel the snake, she could see its intentions. Just on the boundary of its mind, she could feel its malevolence, its innate desire to simply gather its targets together, to crush them and swallow them. Not a complicated creature but a patient and strong one.

She drove harder within her mind looking for that place where she could take control and then she saw her own face in front of her. It looked terrified, but it looked determined. The snake was swaying and she felt the intent to strike. It snapped forward, and she lashed out a thought at it. *"Left."* The fangs swept past her head on her right hand side. It struck again. *"Right."* This time the hissing head swung past her left hand side. She took a moment, recovering. But then it came straight at her.

Scarlett yelled. The snake reared hissing in agony. Stuck in its mind, Scarlett felt like her brain was expanding, bubbling white hot. Her vision was racing, and she realised the snake's head was thrashing about. From the edge of her vision, she saw Rodriguez drop from its coiled body. She felt something else fall. Wilson!

You shall not have me! This is a Welsh woman, and you shall not have me. She realised this was more at the shadow than the snake but her raging mind was simply forcing out its anger and pain. *Feel it, feel the despair. Be rid of me, try to be rid of me!* From her viewpoint in the snake's mind, she saw the wall ahead that it climbed and then the surrounding view as it swung its head round and round.

And then a moment where she saw it explode, brief moments of bits and pieces of flesh before her eyes.

Opening her own eyes, Scarlett saw the giant body of the snake fall from the ruined wall and thump onto the ground, its neck sporting a bloodied empty space where its head had been. Still hanging from her bonds, she cried, her body shaking from fear and enthrallment. The relief of surviving this deadly foe tainted by the realization she had caused this gruesome destruction.

All her life she had loved animals. All through life she thought them worthy of respect, but now, once again, she had killed another. From her rage, from her mind had come such bitter violence. This was a long way from the zoo at the North of Scotland.

The rage was there. The shadow man had said she had her mother's anger. She was so like her mother, for her mother had been here before ever she was.

A few minutes later she felt her bonds drop, and she fell

to the floor. There was nothing around except the body of the large snake. The elliptical headed men must have taken everything else away. Nothing left behind. It was Rodriguez who had cut her bonds and she helped him drag Wilson's inanimate, battered body back to where the tiltrotor had dropped them. Scarlett was almost too numb to feel the pain. *Where do we go now?*

Rodriguez must have been in contact with someone because the tiltrotor arrived. Now staring out of the strange aircraft's window as it took off to the night, she saw the scene of destruction she had left behind. There had been no clean up yet, and the bodies of a couple of harpies and a large giant snake stood out from the ruins. She had been all rage, scared but all rage. *I'm the zookeeper who puts down all the bad animals.* Scarlett wept.

17

Discussions Over Tea

Scarlett stood motionless, looking across the lake. From the water's edge, she saw a light wind causing ripples across the water. An occasional boat would bob up and down but the weather was stopping any serious sightseeing. Snow was falling heavily, enchanting the scene and making the lakes look so clean and pure.

She had travelled up from the base, leaving behind what she saw as a complete mess. Calandra was in the medical facility, her wounds still smarting. Scarlett hadn't been able to see her, but was told by Rodriguez she would be okay. Wilson was in critical care due to the beating he had received. It was strange with Rodriguez as he seemed to be very detached whilst explaining everyone's issues, but every now and then there'd be a flicker of worry that showed his deep connection with his colleagues. Of course, she may just have been reading him wrong as a mute, he communicated with hands pointing to things, and if essential, by writing things down.

What was she doing here? Everyone else had a commitment to what was happening. But Scarlett wondered if she belonged, after all, she generally seemed to be dispatching fantastic and weird creatures.

A short stroll took her to a small coffeehouse where she ordered and then sat with a pot of tea. This was good. As she sat awaiting the one person who had a grip on her past, she hoped he might be able to shed some light on what was really going on.

As the green parka jacket entered through the door, the face was obscured. Scarlett watched and as he turned to close the door she saw the scraggly hair, something her foster mum would have complained to her about. The combat trousers looked very out of place in what was a quaint coffeehouse. Porcelain mugs and proper teapots did not match the distressed student image. The man shambled up, one foot looking awkward. Sitting down, he looked at Scarlett. For a change, it didn't feel as if she was being objectified, but rather appreciated. Most were generally interested in what she could do, not who she was. The others seemed somehow flawed to her because of this.

"Did you see it?" asked Austerley. "Was it the demon?"

Scarlett nodded, her mind flooding back to that moment the necklace was ripped from her. The hand shooting to her breastbone, the snake's death, it was all still there. Austerley reach forward without any hesitation or belief he was being invasive and pulled her T-shirt down to her breastbone, leaving it fully exposed and stared intently.

"Dammit," said Austerley, "I know that hurts. But they said that you controlled the snake. You're not somebody doing parlour tricks." Austerley smiled. "It's you inside, not the necklace. You were one with the beasts."

"I don't understand this, I don't know where it comes from.

I'm just able to talk to them and just able to get into their heads. I'm just able to."

"Scarlett, relax. This is something you are. You are more than a beautiful woman."

Scarlett's head had been hanging down, crestfallen at having lost the necklace but at Austerley's words she raised her eyes staring into his face. The face was heavily jowled, but she saw something akin to a warm summer. This was someone who connected with what she was. Calandra, for all her protective tendencies, seemed to see Scarlett as some sort of hindrance. Wilson always gave the impression of rather reluctantly having brought her onto the team. But this guy in front of her was happy to have met her. No, not happy—actually delighted! Austerley was beaming from ear to ear, his eyes never having left her face.

"How's Calandra?"

Men. They always have to ask after the fit looking woman. Scarlett's face fell slightly but she shrugged her shoulders in negative fashion, and Austerley didn't reach any further.

"Where's your protection?" asked Scarlett. "I don't see him anywhere."

"My protection? Kirkgordon is not my protector."

"Sorry. I thought it was like me and Calandra. I do all this weird stuff, and she looks after me."

"Weird stuff," spat Austerley. "It's not weird. What you do is not freakish to some of us. We can do things a cut above, and you need to realise that. Extremely gifted, especially you. Calandra is a little bit special, as for Kirkgordon, he's just a foot soldier."

"Really, I thought he was like looking after y..."

Austerley's fist hit the table with such a force it would have cleared the coffeehouse if it had not been just opened and empty. "He's not my protector! He doesn't look after me, dammit, he lost me my bloody foot!"

Scarlett looked in the man's eyes, and instead of being repulsed or afraid, she saw something she liked, she saw the little man standing up to the so-called professionals. *You're fine by me*, she thought to herself, *just bloody fine*. "It keeps coming back to me," said Scarlett, "That demon, the thing was like a fire that ripped into my neck, and it's starting to appear in my dreams."

"You don't have to talk to me about dreams," said Austerley, and he turned his head to look through the window at the lake.

"But it's constantly there, but not him so much as the other one, the shadow. The shadow comes to me in the most bizarre dreams. In dreams where I should be happy, things which should be romantic. Things where I'm with a man, but instead of the man comes this thing, taking away all the pleasure of the feelings, those sorts of feelings," said Scarlett. She was holding back, afraid to show her real repugnance, the violation she felt as she knew if she did, she'd be a quivering wreck in this place.

Austerley reached forward with a hand, staring up into a pained face. "He had contact with you. This is probably what happened with your mother, and we're going to need to prevent it. Being a shadow, he will tail you, he will follow you, and he is part of you now unless we get rid of it. The others, Wilson, Calandra and bloody Kirkgordon, they'll be concerned about the demon, not about this. But for you, this is the real threat, this shadow. We need to find it and kill off the shadow once and for all.

"We?" asked Scarlett. "You'll help me?"

Austerley smiled. "I'll help you, but we're going to have to get past Kirkgordon on this one. He likes orders, he likes to see where things have come from, and he'll see this as a key mission. We'll have to sell it to him."

"You said that he wasn't your protector?"

"He's not my protector. But he is my partner, and we do go places together to sort things out." Austerley grimaced. "I suppose he's handy in a fight. But he doesn't appreciate these things we delve into. And he's also got another side too. I don't call him 'Churchy' for no reason."

"Churchy? You mean like the chapel."

"He's one of these believers. Not that it seems to have helped his wife," said Austerley. "He sees the things before us as evil, as wrong. Things not to be touched, never to be explored or controlled."

"My step family went to chapel. I never understood fully all the smells and bells and this and that," Scarlett said. "There have been times when I have had feelings about the shadow which have caused me to pray. But it's kind of hard thinking about that stuff when I can talk to animals like I'm Dr. Doolittle's wife."

"We need to work out how to trap it. In fact, how to destroy it."

Their thoughts were interrupted as the waitress came over asking if they were ready to order. Austerley muttered something, obviously annoyed at being interrupted and Scarlett had to order for both of them. They both sat in silence before the order arrived. The waitress was trying her best to give exemplary service, but Austerley wasn't bothered and eventually grunted at her to leave. Scarlett apologized. *He's quite highly strung.*

When the waitress had disappeared, Austerley took one of the cups and reached inside his jacket for a substance that Scarlett didn't recognize. Austerley mixed the substance in the cup with a little bit of liquid from the teapot trying to make sure no one else could see what was happening. Scarlett's amusement at his action changed to wonder as fumes began to form over the flat surface above the cup, and she began to see images. Austerley was chanting under his breath and his hands moved making complex patterns before eventually he seemed to come to rest and fixed on the smokescreen in front of them.

Scarlett saw flashes in the black, heads, elliptical in shape. Austerley was fixated on this changing vapour before him and she noted every time the image changed his hands had flicked slightly. He was also controlling it somehow, searching for something. "What is it you're trying to get?" she asked.

"Shush," whispered Austerley.

Watching his eyes race across every image, she became engrossed in this man in front of her. She always thought that she would like one of these musclebound hunks and a noted upstanding man but here she was looking at someone that could be mistaken for a tramp. But he had such purpose, such a desire to help her. She recalled Calandra telling her that she was with Austerley, but he couldn't love her in the way that others had, but as a freak, not a woman. But for Scarlett, it had been the opposite. *Everybody else just wanted something from this freak, but he wants to help me, wants to sort this out for me. He's been kinder than any of them.*

Turning back to the picture, it seemed to be concentrating on the shadow man. He was there, in every image. Moving here, moving there in the dark along walls, amongst different pieces of furniture or floors. Never seen fully, but his presence was a constant, heavy weight on the mind. Scarlett's heart was racing. She looked at the shadow that had come in the recent nightmare events, the one who had given her the creeps back in the runes then at the sacrifice.

"I know the plan," said Austerley. "I damn well know what it wants, and I know where it is going."

"Really? You can tell that from just what you saw."

Austerley looked up. His face seemed to begin to fall into a scowl but then a smile came across his lips. "Yes," he said "Yes, I can. You didn't mean that negatively, did you? You were just kind of impressed?"

"Impressed? More than impressed. I'm just grateful that's all. It's amazing, quite amazing."

Austerley looked like he was about to explode with pride, and hunching forward again, took Scarlett's hands. "I know where to find the shadow man, he's being sent to pick up the next creature. I know what it is, but the creature will be difficult, very difficult. Now the demon has arrived, it seems that mere harpies are not enough to protect it. It's been messed around with. It wants something bigger, it wants to command things larger before it begins its attack."

"Its attack?"

"Yes, its attack on the world. It will gather these creatures and it will attack the world," said Austerley as if this was the most obvious and mundane fact ever. "Demons want chaos. They want rack and ruin. It's what they do." Again, Austerley's face was that of someone who had just announced that ice cream was cold. Obvious and not just to himself, surely to everyone.

"This demon, it's bringing up a creature that's somehow

worse than what we've seen so far?"

Austerley nodded. "It's one from the deep. Ever heard of a Kraken?"

"Yes. The beast from beneath the waves, it drags down ships to Davy Jones locker."

"That's it, but that's a much sanitized version for children really. The demon is going to raise it for a private army of creatures. The trouble with a Kraken," said Austerley, "is it doesn't tend to rise up easily when summoned, which means that when summoned it can be a bother to put back down. And if he has it moving about the water as opposed to residing in the deep, we will need some help. We need something big enough to deal with a Kraken, to give it a blow. The only thing I can think of at the moment is something I don't want to go to. But you'll be able to deal with it."

"I will?"

"It's intelligent and clever, but you can work around it."

Scarlett was in wonder. What were they going to see? But she also blushed at the compliment. She found her hands gripping his tightly.

"You've got an old friend to see. It'll be a couple of days' travel, to the Andes, and high up. Been a long time since they flew around the earth, a long, long time. She is very old. You met one of her offspring, I think."

"Her offspring? Did I?"

"Yes, the offspring is your firebird, Flame. We need to pick it up from the base."

"She's getting treatment, like Calandra."

"She doesn't need to be in total shape," said Austerley, "but she needs to see her with you, that you are respected by the firebird. You have to control the mind of this one."

"She's not coming. Flame is hurt, she needs to recover." Scarlett shot down Austerley's look that was telling her the opposite.

Austerley became rather grim. "You'll have to win its trust on your own then, have to believe in what you're going to do and it's probably best that I take a slightly backward role." He looked sheepishly out the window.

"Why is that?" asked Scarlett.

"Kind of broke the legs of its child last time," said Austerley, "Didn't really go down well."

Scarlett laughed. There was something about this man, something to warm to.

"The other thing is," said Austerley, "the demon will rise in the shadows. At the moment it is limited, but it will grow to full strength in six months. In the meantime, it will assemble an army, but will do it through the shadow man. He's his right-hand man. If we eliminate him, we can slow down the demon. I need to get Churchy, he needs to be briefed on this."

Scarlett watched Austerley amble away, and the waitress came up asking if she wanted anything else. Scarlett quickly waved her hand, indicating the same again, but there was a beaming smile on her face. The waitress was amused. Once her new drink arrived, Scarlett drank deeply from the hot liquid whilst looking out of the window. The last week had not been what she would have ever wished for, but this guy…well, he seemed like an adventure worth having.

Someone was sitting in front of her. She hadn't seen him arrive or heard him, but he was now sitting in front of her. It was the man who had been up on the mountain, the man Calandra had stopped to talk to. He seemed quite annoyed. Austerley was there too and sat down beside Scarlett. There were no pleasantries from the new arrival, rather he was very direct.

"To get this straight, she needs to go and pick up a creature and then we need to take on something that comes out of the deep. That right?"

Austerley nodded.

"What creature are we picking up?" asked the man.

"Austerley knows," said Scarlett.

"You mean, Indy hasn't told you what it is?" said the man, rolling his eyes.

"Indy?" asked Scarlett.

"Yes, Indiana Jones here, after anything of any culture as long as it's dark, mysterious and probably ending the world. Dabbler in the worst of things."

"That's a bit rude," said Scarlett, "considering what he does, considering he looks after you."

"He looks after me? You know I'm the bodyguard. I'm here to make sure he doesn't get into trouble."

"Bollocks," said Scarlett, "he looks like he can handle himself to me."

"Yes, Churchy," said Austerley, "I can handle myself."

"You don't get it, Scarlett, I'm not here to protect him from other things. I'm here to protect him from himself. He nearly caused the end of the world."

"But I put that demon back."

"And you summoned it in the first place. He causes havoc wherever he goes. Something if you stick around you'll find out. I'm here to make sure the world gets back to one piece."

"And that you do so well," laughed Austerley. "Top leader, never a cross word, never a dull moment."

Kirkgordon ignored Austerley. "So, where to this time?"

asked Kirkgordon, "which mouth of hell are we disappearing into?"

"South America," said Austerley. "We'll need to go onto somewhere else after the Andes to see if things are happening. But first, a stop off to see an old friend. One that might not be so happy about seeing me."

"And this has come from Wilson, has it?" said Kirkgordon.

"Well things ain't that simple. Wilson's injured, Calandra's indisposed. That's why we need you. It's important. I know what needs done."

Kirkgordon shook his head and got up from his chair, turned his back and started to walk away. But then he stopped deep in contemplation before coming back to the table.

"Just for the record I don't believe a word of this, but if *he*," Kirkgordon pointed at Austerley, "thinks it's important, let's get it done."

Kirkgordon turned around and walked off, never looking back. Looking up at Austerley, she saw a smile. *I hope I know what I'm doing. God knows what's coming next.*

18

The Dragon

Three days of constant travelling, and Scarlett was exhausted from the moment they had been forced to run to get the flight across continents. Sitting for hours in the back of the plane, inching into one another for lack of space, and each time the plane decreased in size. They then boarded a train and lastly ended up in this pickup truck of sorts. The whole trip they had been on the go from day one. It was a bit of a whirlwind apart from the times when they feasted at some dodgy food court.

For once she was the centre of attention, completely the focus. Austerley was still dressed in his camouflage trousers and Parker jacket, and he did nothing but regale her about the numerous and varied marvellous things he had seen in his lifetime. All the time he was doing it, he would hold her hand or encourage her gently. On the other hand, Kirkgordon was very abrupt, always looking around them, rarely at them. In some ways he reminded her of Calandra, but he was more on edge, constantly checking.

At one point, Scarlett had mentioned to him that it must

be a bit exciting living this life, travelling with Austerley. "One bloody lunatic" was the reply, and when she questioned Austerley about it, he mentioned that Kirkgordon's wife was undergoing some issues with things that had happened.

Scarlett had never been in South America, and as she headed up into the mountains in the pickup truck, she'd been forced to sit beside Kirkgordon. Austerley had planned to sit in the back with Scarlett, but as Kirkgordon pointed out Austerley knew the way, he didn't and secondly, there was an important person to look after and protect, Scarlett, in the rear and that stupid, fat arse can look after himself in the front. Scarlett sensed some antagonism between the two guys, but she did wonder how bad it really was. *Austerley seems so charming. Sure, at times he was a bit patronising, but that was because people didn't understand him when he explained things that weren't simple. He was certainly very engaging with her.*

As the truck continued to jostle about on the potholed road into the middle of who knows where, Scarlett reached out again to Kirkgordon.

"That's it, gone ten. Well, ten their time. I'm all over the place."

"You never get used to time zoning. Hopefully we won't be too long, but it depends on his nibs up the front. He's been muttering about where it is and where it was. After spending a lot of time with him, I'm used to this nonsense."

"He seems quite knowledgeable about all this. Seems to really understand it."

"Understand? Maybe, but more like steeped in it, delighted. He used to be a mental patient." Scarlett raised her eyebrows. "It's true. For a whole year he was a mental patient, absolutely doolally. Pray we don't hear any gunfire."

"What happened that he ended up getting out of the Institute?"

"He was released by a shape shifting dragon and the two of us went on a wild goose chase around the world. In the end, he nearly destroyed it. The world, that is."

"You keep alluding to the fact he nearly ended the world. That doesn't seem like something he would…"

"He nearly ended the world for Calandra. Just be careful, he's probably giving you a lot of attention at the moment. Just be very careful, my wife is in an institution because of him. There's part of him wants to do the right thing, but there is another part, so curious, so desperate to know and to engage with things that are best kept under the carpet, that if you are around for too long, it will affect you."

Scarlett felt quite aggrieved at the attack on her admirer. *He seems so charming. It's only been a few days but he's very attentive, very interested. This guy is just so bitter.* She looked and saw the back of Austerley's head, the unkempt hair bobbing about as the truck pitched here and there. She turned back to Kirkgordon. "He doesn't seem to have affected you much anyway."

Kirkgordon turned his head slowly and looked straight at her. She watched him roll back the sleeve of his jacket to reveal the bare flesh of the arm. She was startled when the arm opened, two panels moving mechanically to one side, and then from the middle appeared a small crossbow. It came to rest atop the arm and the panels closed back over. "No, he hasn't affected me at all, has he?" said Kirkgordon, tone sarcastic to the core. "I used to be able to draw a bow, I was a damn good archer but I can't hold the bow any more. Too many tremors."

"Why? What happened?"

"I was hung over a precipice. There was something that could destroy the world coming in from another dimension at the time and we were in another dimension, another world. Calandra had gone all ice. It's something you may have seen her do, but this was beyond how she normally is. Meanwhile Austerley was trying to sort it all out. We were hanging, all three of us, over a precipice and this thing from the dark grabbed her by the ankles. I was hanging onto her when she went all ice. Froze my arms."

He hung his head looking deep in thought. "Quite brilliant really, the surgeons, but although they put me back together, I don't feel in the same way with the arm. I get sensations, I get certain things. I can operate the arm but I don't feel with it like I do with the other one. And it scares my kids. I guess I'm just a freak like him now, part of Austerley's freak show."

And it dawned on Scarlett, *I'm part of this freak show too.*

"You seem sensible," continued Kirkgordon as he turned, giving a smile that then faded. "Be very careful before you get involved in this freak show. I can't walk out. I'm in too deep but you haven't even started yet. Just be careful."

"It has wounded me as well," said Scarlett, pulling down her top to show the gorged scar along her breastbone.

"It does look sore, but that's just a flesh wound. To hold yourself sane," he laughed, "and together, you need to have a grounding. You need to have something; you need to have a faith. There was a time when the blackness came into my mind, blackness by the way that was in Austerley's foot." Scarlett looked quizzical, not quite understanding what she was hearing. "A dark poison he had taken into his foot, taken from someone else. Yes, you can look at me like that. It is strange, it is bizarre, it is nuts. But that's why I'm warning you. I know you're Welsh, but did you ever have a faith when in Wales?"

"My foster parents took me to chapel," said Scarlett, "I was brought up in chapel, was there every Sunday. Like a good Catholic."

Kirkgordon smiled. "Then that's your anchor." He reached round to the back of his neck and removed something from under his jacket. She watched him take a gold necklace with a cross on the front which he reached over to place around her neck. Fixing its clasp, he said, "If you only think of one thing when it goes dark remember this. Just remember this."

His voice was deadly earnest as she watched him stare at the cross now hanging down from her neck. There was no feeling of this being a leer. Despite it being at the top of her cleavage, he was lost in that little gold symbol at the end of the chain. After a moment, he turned around and stared out into the rapidly increasing foliage around them.

Scarlett placed a hand on the cross. It had been a long time since she'd thought about Him. A very long time since she'd been in the place of prayer or anything spiritual. Still, the sentiment was nice. At least he did seem to care.

The pickup truck bounced along for another half an hour before stopping abruptly. Austerley stepped out of the front of the vehicle and merely nodded at Kirkgordon in the rear. He then turned and went over to a piece of foliage, studying intently. The driver came round to Kirkgordon and said something in a language Scarlett didn't recognise. It was clear Kirkgordon didn't recognise the language either and decided to call over Austerley to find out what the man had said. Without turning around, Austerley called back that he wanted payment.

Scarlett continued to watch Austerley as Kirkgordon handed over some money, and the pickup truck pulled away. It was like he was in a trance, some sort of a dream.

"Are we gonna do something?" said Kirkgordon. Austerley nodded. But he then stood looking more intently in front of them. "Today, Indy?"

"What this arse doesn't realise is that," said Austerley, giving a dismissive wave at Kirkgordon, "this plant doesn't come from the earth. This plant, as opposed to that plant, and every other plant around here, comes from a place where the creature comes from. The place where the creature stays most of the time, its shelter from the world."

"The creature?" asked Scarlett. "Is it big or small? I can't see any creature around here."

"That's because it's inside the mountain," said Austerley. "It's deep inside the mountain, but this is a way to get to it. Mind though, it's clever. It's a very clever creature, its intelligence will be up and around that of you and I, but far higher than Kirkgordon's. So be very careful as you will not simply enter its mind. You'll have to debate with it, to talk to it, best it. Then you will have to dominate it at all times otherwise we'll end up being toast."

"Toast?" said Kirkgordon, "Flames then, some sort of hot breath? Is this another bloody dragon?"

Austerley nodded.

"A dragon," said Scarlett, "There was a dragon over the car Calandra crashed. I sent it away. It wasn't difficult."

"No, that one might not have been, but this will be," said Austerley. "Some of them are just creatures but some of them have real minds of their own and can do things you don't understand."

"You mean like Farthington?" asked Kirkgordon. "This had better not end up in another end of the world scenario."

"It's already an end of the world scenario," said Austerley. "That demon is loose, which means it's an end of the world scenario. This is what we deal with. It's why they need me involved."

"Need you involved? It's usually you that makes it an end of the world scenario. And it's me that's needed to make sure your arse ends up on the right side of it."

"Do you two always bicker like this?" snapped Scarlett. "It's bloody annoying. Where's the dragon? Where am I going?"

"This way," said Austerley, pushing aside the leaf he was looking at. "This way, because the clever one will have to lead the way."

Scarlett heard a tut from Kirkgordon, but he never focused on her or Austerley, instead his gaze was always on the surroundings, whatever else was going on. *I guess he is a protector, a bit like Calandra. That's where I'm seeing the connection. They are very similar.* And then it struck. *Does that make me like Austerley? Am I an end-of-the-world scenario?*

Scarlett began to sweat copiously on the way up the mountainside. The green vegetation became denser, and they started to see little insects on every leaf. The ground beneath seemed also to move at times with swarms of creatures. She could hear all their voices, but she was pushing them back. All these busy insects meant too many minds all at once. One large animal, that was easier to deal with. And there was a single mind out there. There was a presence, something on the edge of her consciousness that she was struggling to pick up.

"How far?" asked Kirkgordon.

"Close," answered Scarlett. "Close."

She saw Austerley look at her with a pleasant smile. "She's right, it'll be just through here. I think I can see a path."

"If there's a path, it's incredibly faint," remarked Scarlett, but she followed Austerley regardless. They reached a great grey slab in the mountainside. On it were certain figures and shapes but they were not a language she recognised. Kirkgordon took one look at it and turned his back to take up what seemed to be a defensive position while Austerley approached the stone looking thoughtful. Scarlett tried to speak, but Austerley raised his hand indicating he wanted silence. But a voice in her head came questioning.

Who are you? Why are you here? I know that you can hear me.

Scarlett thought about replying back, decided against it, and chose to tell the boys something didn't seem to be welcoming. However, Austerley was in mid-chant murmuring something, his hands waving over the grey stone in front of them so she remained quiet. Scarlett watched the symbols on the door begin to ignite, coming alive with an orange and the door was gone. It had simply vanished. Austerley turned, smiled and then stepped forward. On hearing his footsteps, Kirkgordon turned slowly and nodded an indication at Scarlett, instructing her to follow Austerley.

Inside was dark and the air was clammy. Scarlett found herself sweating even more than she thought she could. *I wish I was more fit. Kirkgordon's barely feeling anything. Oh my, Austerley's dripping.* Looking back at the doorway behind them, she saw it was now closed over again with a large stone.

The tunnel was short, which was good. There seemed to be light coming from up ahead but how could that be? The tunnel broke out into a vast area that seemed bigger than the mountain itself. And she heard the voice again. *Why are you here? What do you want? Do you know who I am?*

There was a swish in the vegetation ahead and Scarlett was reminded of being in the car with Calandra that was singed by the dragon. That feeling just before… She felt someone grabbing her shoulder and then was dragged into the undergrowth with no time to stare at the fabulous fauna and flowers that raced past her face. Austerley, however, stood out in the open and began shouting in a language Scarlett didn't understand. She lay huddled in the undergrowth with Kirkgordon but could see the scaled beast with enormous talons that landed ahead of Austerley. It was about the size of a London double-decker bus, but its tail stretched out much further. It was golden in colour and stared at Austerley. Its long neck swung down, bringing its head right before Austerley's face. Austerley was still talking to it in some language. And then the dragon spoke back in what passed for the same language.

"Austerley, what are you doing? What's it saying?" asked Kirkgordon.

"Just told me not to try and do that spell. It won't work, which is kind of a problem. That was plan A."

"What's plan B?" said Kirkgordon.

"I was kind of hoping that plan A would work."

Kirkgordon leapt from the undergrowth, his arm opening up and producing the crossbow through his jacket. He aimed a bolt, loosing it straight at the creature's head. The dragon turned and the bolt glanced off its skin, disappearing into the distance.

"Bollocks!" said Kirkgordon, running for cover as the

dragon's head swept round and a tongue of fire poured out. Scarlett watched Kirkgordon roll away, covering himself in a ball made of his jacket. The fire blazed over the top of him, and she gasped fearing the worst. Then he leapt back up, much to the dragon's, and Scarlett's, surprise.

"Where did you get that hide?" roared the dragon.

"Is not my fault. You shed your skin," shouted Kirkgordon, "It's not like I killed for it."

"It does not matter, I will crush you, and I will crush your friend."

"I can believe it. Maybe we should try something different." Kirkgordon produced something from underneath his jacket and threw it into the air. There was a blinding flash and Scarlett found herself unable to see. She heard a roar from the dragon, and a yell from Kirkgordon. At first it sounded like a yell of victory then it was a cry, and the ground around her shook as something moved. As her eyes slowly adjusted from the blinding light, she saw a large clawed foot in the foliage. But the owner's attention was on Austerley.

"And now, what do we do with you?" said the dragon, "maybe a simple crushing?"

It looked hopeless but Scarlett needed the dragon to stop. She stood up and threw her jacket down, sweat pouring off of her. The heat was oppressive. The whole situation was oppressive. And Austerley was staring at a fire breathing dragon which looked enormous.

Stepping out of the undergrowth, Scarlett shouted to get the dragon's attention and its head spun round immediately. She could hear a voice.

You! You are here. It's been too long. Why are you here with them? Why have you brought them here? What have I done to offend you that you bring this to me?

I don't know you, thought Scarlett, *I've never met you.*

Never met? Never met? But we were so close, and then you went, never came back. You used to fly on me, we would go places. Where did you go? I missed you, Cerys, I missed you.

Cerys, Cerys, that's a Welsh name. Who's Cerys? asked Scarlett.

The dragon grabbed Austerley and laid him on the ground before placing a foot over him. *Maybe it's the passage of time or maybe the light of the mountain but you look as she looked. You have Cerys' face, her hair. She could not handle the heat either, always sweated like you, but she always came back to see me. I helped her do things, solve things and then it changed when she had a little one. She brought her little one here once but visits were rare after that. She said she had to be on the move too often but that was twenty or so of your earth years, twenty of these things, what you call time passing. But you look like Cerys.*

The dragon reached for her with a claw. Scarlett shook as it touched a talon down the side of her face. It was hard and slightly rough. The golden talon then delicately reached down and pulled forward her T-shirt. She watched the large eyes look at her scar.

You are like her, you are a fire inside like her. Passionate, impulsive. Maybe obstinate too. And they have hurt you. You have been hurt. The large talon gently lifted Scarlett's face so her eyes were staring straight into the dragon's. *You are hers. My friend. My dear, dear friend. You are hers! Cerys was your mother.*

19

The Search

Scarlett felt the wind making her hair bustle as they glided amongst the clouds. It was quite bizarre being on the back of the dragon, especially with the boys behind her, sitting in manufactured seats. It struck her that as well as the leather binding which went around the dragon just at the end of its neck, that they were sitting almost on its main body. On the other hand, Scarlett was right up on its head, no harness on at all, almost attached to it. It was as if her skin and that of the dragon at her hand became one, almost melting into the flesh. When it had first taken off, it had taken some time to get used to as she looked around at the rapidly vanishing ground below. She worried about falling off as they were going this way and that, causing her to feel sick until the dragon spoke to her, and she moved into its mind to be one with the Dragon. Scarlett saw through the dragon's eyes, seeing far to the west and east, seeing with incredible clarity little boats at an island far, far below. Truly, she was one with it, and it was truly one with her.

As they travelled, it was telling her things about her mother, long treasured memories. For her mother would come and spend months of her time in that hidden land inside the mountain. He spoke of the joy the two of them had, a higher creature with such a mind that he was able to speak with as an equal. Many of those whom it could converse with had wanted its golden dragon skin, and its very life was always under threat. As an example, it mentioned Kirkgordon's coat which Scarlett had thought was a basic leather but which turned out to be dragon hide. Thankfully, Scarlett found on asking that Kirkgordon's hide was shed from a dragon's skin, not from something captured. Although working for the company, Scarlett found Kirkgordon to have his own standards and morals.

Austerley was something else. Kirkgordon had been more than clear about Austerley's issues, about the difficulties in working with him, but there was still something attractive to it. For one, he was here without hesitation. Also the things he could do with the doorway into the giant cave. All this madness didn't seem to faze him, although he was quite an amusing figure and in the fashion sense, he was a disaster. He had also been a bit queasy on the dragon, asking to go lower constantly which was inevitably followed by murmurs of "shut up" from Kirkgordon.

It was not that Kirkgordon was immune to trials of flight but was more intent on what was ahead to think about being sick. Austerley was required to steer, so to speak, as only he had a notion of where this new beast would appear, a beast he said which would be much, much larger and which was why they required a dragon. While Scarlett wished that Calandra was here, as she seemed much more normal than the two boys, she remembered her foster mom saying *you get what you get and you get on with it.*

She had come a long way since the days of the Welsh valleys, boys teasing her at school because of her stumpy but buxom figure, the days of trying to make a life in the mundane jobs that she'd worked. Now, here she was talking to a dragon, a beast master. As a rule, she always kicked hard, but her new abilities meant she punched well above her size now. And the more she learned of her mother from this dragon, the more she was sure she could play the role. Her mother had possessed a sophisticated style of dress, the dragon had said, complete with cape. It had sounded very 1970's, but when she had seen the actual garment, she had taken to it immediately. On the outside, jet black and when she was wrapped up in it, the cape gave off a sleek finish which, hopefully, covered all those lumps that she didn't want seen.

The particular cape she was wearing had been left by her mother with the dragon, who believed she should have a number of them in different places. There was also a hat that was tucked away inside the cape so as not to lose it on the flight, and then there was the pair of riding boots which came up to her thighs. In some ways, they seemed wholly ridiculous for at the top of them were large lapels, thick chunks of leather that stuck out around, but which were carefully trimmed between the thighs, making walking easy.

When she dressed in these clothes, the dragon was obviously very excited and kept telling her she looked like her mother. Austerley also watched her a lot. It felt good to be admired in that way but also because she felt like she was the dominant one in it. In all honesty, the outfit needed worked on because her thighs inside the boots were very tight and she wasn't that sure they would come off that easy, unless she let someone else remove them. And the cape wasn't really an everyday wear. She wondered if it was just some sort of fashion statement or did it really have a purpose, but the dragon was insistent that the interior had various pockets, all of which seemed to be empty.

One of the other things she learned from the dragon about her mother, which surprised her, was the poster inside the dragon's cave. On the interior of the cave, there was a seemingly random film poster of "Gone with the Wind". Her mother had loved that film and the poor dragon had been forced to watch it with her repeatedly. Scarlett had always wondered why she had her name when she was so blonde. Now it made sense.

At Austerley's insistence, the dragon dived down to be low over the ocean, and Scarlett sensed a panic at the rear of the flight. Scarlett was immersed in the dragon's mind and thrilled as they dropped out of the sky, spinning and looping, before beginning to glide. The wings beat ever so gently as they flew close to the sea, close enough to watch the sun reflect off of it. Then at a small piece of land, an island not much bigger than a play park, the dragon set down easily onto what was a rocky outlet. The small piece of beach to one side had water lapping up, but there were no trees, nothing to stop the heat of the blazing sun. In flight, she had been cool enough, but down at rest, Scarlett felt the heat come down.

"Where are we?" asked Scarlett. She watched Austerley, still holding his stomach and looking as if he was about to be sick.

"Middle of the ocean, east of the Falklands by a fair bit." Austerley disappeared behind the rocky outcrop and the sound of spewing was heard.

"Can you see anything around? I saw nothing up there,"

asked Kirkgordon.

"Nothing around," said Scarlett.

Yes, there is! It was the dragon talking to Scarlett. *Ahead there is something. A ship, out to what you would see as the west. It's quite large, flat middle, houses at one end. I can't read any writing on the side at this distance. But it does seem to have an awful lot of decayed sides to it. Rust? Is that your word?*

Scarlett nodded and the dragon signalled its acknowledgement and continued to stare right into the distance. Emerging from behind the rock and looking very much the worse for wear, Austerley began to look out towards the sea.

"It will be from that direction, somewhere over there," said Austerley.

"Care to narrow it down, Indy?"

"He's right, Kirkgordon. The dragon has seen something out there. A boat, it said it was large and flat. Very rusty. Sounds like some sort of tanker."

"Rusty? Mmm…" said Kirkgordon, "Can't guarantee that it's what we're looking for."

"Can you not feel it?" Austerley asked. "From the deep?" Still looking at Scarlett, he saw her shake her head.

"I feel nothing but this dragon beside me."

Austerley nodded and then stepped closer to the water's edge looking out in the same direction. "They are out there, they come up from beneath."

Kirkgordon laughed. "So something is out there and we're not sure what, but this something is going to do something, which hasn't happened yet, and which we haven't a clue about? Just great. Don't think we need to debate this much more. That's the only thing near here, and Austerley's water is up. But we need to be near…"

"The platform of the boat," said Austerley. "Get me down on the boat."

"Yes, I thought of that blinding idea too," said Kirkgordon. "We can sneak up on this boat, on the back of a golden dragon in broad daylight and descend onto the boat. They'll never see us!"

"There is no need to be sarcastic," said Scarlett.

"Actually, I have a right to be sarcastic," said Kirkgordon, "as it's a kamikaze job. It's bloody obvious that it's going to be hard to be effective as we are going in completely open. And what exactly are we going to have waiting for us?"

"The men," said Austerley. "The legacy of the abandoned men from Innsmouth, I think."

"Innsmouth?" asked Scarlett.

"The elliptical headed people you've seen. They're from a church of sorts. American originally but now scattered," said Kirkgordon. "These guys will be halfway to being frogmen."

"Frogmen?"

"Yes," said Austerley, "Frogmen, fish-heads, a transformation due to the god they worshipped. He actually comes from afar, a different place in space and maybe time. These guys have changed from the normal pattern. They must have a different headship. There's been no symbols that indicate they would be Dagon followers, but the shape of their heads. And being involved with this demon is not their way. No, this will be different."

"Okay, so elliptical headed guys," said Scarlett. "Anyone else gonna be there?"

"The shadow, Scarlett, the shadow will be there. He's been there all the other times commanding."

"Okay," said Kirkgordon, "Let's get cracking hopefully we

can stop whatever they are and whatever it is before it arrives."

"Not that simple, Churchy," said Austerley. "The problem is that if we go beforehand, you may be able to stop them, but there's nothing to say that they won't come back and wake it up again. I need to see the place. I need to see him coming up to put an end to this chapter."

"So we need to just wait and hold off until they get up whatever's coming up from the deep," asked Kirkgordon. "Bloody magic, it's always the same. Why can't it just be a case of closing the door? No, we have to let them open it so we know where to close it. Oh, and you guys might as well have a turn with whatever's coming out first. That's not a plan, Indy, that's a suicide mission. Bloody typical."

Do they always argue like this?

Yes, Scarlett thought back, *they seem to. What were you thinking? Any ideas on how to approach this?*

The man with the weapon in his arm is right. There will be a poor chance of survival if they raise up whatever they are looking for. Things from the deep are often powerful. I don't think it's a good idea then, if your friend is going to put it back, that we are on the boat. We can probably drop them on the boat and hopefully they can defend themselves. You and I should keep to the air where I have an advantage, and I can use my fire. And your mother talked about the shadow man. It was never good.

The dragon's strategic thoughts were interrupted by Kirkgordon. "We might as well have some food around here while waiting." He strode into the water until he was about knee deep, glanced around him before pointing down towards a patch of water. His arm opened up and the small crossbow appeared. Loaded into it was a bolt. He looked again at the water, fired, before stepping forward to pull something out of the water. It was a sort of large fish, but Scarlett didn't know the type.

"Pointless," said Austerley, "unless you like sushi that's not going be much use."

Kirkgordon ignored the jibe and placed the fish on a rock. He took a small knife, lopped off the head, gutted it, cut out fillets from either side and draped them on another piece of rock. "Scarlett, get your friend to light a fire over it."

There were no words. Scarlett knew the dragon was already on its way to ever so gently send a blade of flame over the fish. She watched it cook over the next minute and a half until the fillets were ready to flip. The white flesh looked good.

Kirkgordon took a third of the fish and handed it to Scarlett, before picking up another third for himself. He sat down on the beach, muttering to Austerley that his was there on the plate. Austerley grumbled but moved over and started to eat the fish. The dragon in the meantime looked out to sea noting to Scarlett that the boat had stopped but there was little activity on it and certainly no activity in the water.

Night eventually began to fall and the heat of the day dissipated beneath cloudless skies. Scarlett lay back in the sand, looking up at the sky, seeing the stars twinkling brightly. She was amazed at the heavens and wrapped her cloak tighter around herself due to the chill, but nothing put off her investigations of the glimmering lights up there in the heavens. It reminded her of a tapestry back in her local chapel. A figure laid down beside her. She turned her head expecting to see Austerley but it was Kirkgordon instead.

"Takes my breath away as well," he said. "It doesn't happen much back home. Rarely do we get such clear skies, but when we do, I like nothing better than to lay down outside and look up. It's much simpler really." Scarlett just nodded and returned to her musings on the sky.

There's something, came the dragon's voice in her head, interrupting her thoughts. Scarlett got to her feet.

"What's up?" asked Kirkgordon.

"He sees something, he sees something," said Scarlett excitedly.

There is movement, said the dragon, *people on the edge of the boat, entering into the water.*

"Anything going into the water?" asked Austerley almost giddily.

Someone's been put into the water, I think bound. Not going in of their own accord, said the dragon.

"They're putting people in. Bound up, sacrifice maybe?" suggested Scarlett.

"It begins," said Austerley. "We need to get over there, that's the sacrifice, that's the calling of the Kraken."

Scarlett was amused at the speed with which Austerley moved to get himself onto the harness of the dragon. Kirkgordon was shaking his head at this but nonetheless took Scarlett's hand to climb a rocky outcrop onto the dragon. Swinging its head around, the dragon let Kirkgordon scramble up its body into his position.

"Don't get too close and don't hold back with what you can do," said Kirkgordon. "These men are as far away from people as possible. Going to be merry hell once we're on board. Scarlett, whatever happens, don't worry about us, don't worry about anything except putting that Kraken back in and getting rid of these people who called it. This is an endgame, and we have to end it. For if this creature is as terrible as Austerley says, we sure don't want the demon to have it."

Scarlett looked briefly at Austerley who seemed to come alive. He was almost giddy with excitement, and Scarlett turned back and fell into the dragon's mind again, becoming as one. Her eyes were its eyes and with a thought she told it to take-off.

Jumping from the rocks below, the beast flew up into the air, climbing to get height as it made its way towards the boat. Scarlett, through the dragon's eyes, saw the people on the vessel looking over the side, throwing things in, chanting, and saying things that were inaudible. They seemed to be manic, so many different people, but there was a leader of sorts. A man in a strange outfit had some sort of sceptre that he was waving about. Maybe Austerley would know what it was about when they got there. The far side of the tanker was fairly empty as most of the people gathered around the edge were looking into the water. Although dark, the night was very clear due to the full moon in the sky.

Turning around, she told the boys to get ready and then back in the dragon again, assumed its mind into her. The great beast flew high above the vessel now and right over the side of the vessel that was reasonably devoid of men. She heard a cry from Austerley as the dragon dove down before landing lightly on the deck. The boys dropped off the great creature, and it spring back to the air on hearing Kirkgordon call clear.

Climbing back up, she looked behind to see what looked like an octopus limb arcing out from the sea. From far below, she could hear Austerley's cry of "Kraken" split the air. There were explosions from below inside the boat. Turning the dragon back round, she saw Kirkgordon standing in front of Austerley but firing off all sorts of small items. There were explosions and smoke in the general melee and dozens of elliptical headed men raced towards him. But there were also large black tentacles reaching around the boat now.

Austerley had begun to shout-chant, and he was milling his arms around, but Scarlett could see one of the Kraken limbs heading towards him. Kirkgordon threw something at it which exploded, but was then knocked aside by one of the limbs that continued towards Austerley.

Scarlett drove the dragon down and erupted fire on the limb. Smelling the cooking flesh of the Kraken, she was shocked that the limb was still moving along but had at least released its grip on Austerley. She saw Kirkgordon get to his feet, dragging Austerley for cover down into the vessel itself, toward what seemed like the cargo holds. Passing by the side of the boat, she reared violently as a large head erupted from the sea, a bulbous octopus-like head with red eyes. She was taken aback and the dragon flew up, turning aside, straight into one of the tentacle limbs which wrapped itself round the dragon. Scarlett felt the pain, felt the cry from the creature which raged fire all around in a desperate bid to reach its attacker. It was only moments, just moments, before she felt the cold water on her face, and they were dragged under.

20

The Kraken

The water was cold on Scarlett's face, and she felt herself fighting hard, trying to push back to the surface. She thought about letting go of the dragon and swimming up. Her mind was still connected and she could feel the squeeze of the tentacle. The dragon tried in its situation to roar out a blaze of fire but found itself choking on the water rushing in on it. This was a different medium. There on land it was a deadly beast, even in the air, but here under the water it was struggling, its wings useless, more of a hindrance and its main weapon of fire gone.

Scarlett reached out with her mind to try to connect with the Kraken. Always black. More than black. She started to feel the repressive evil seeping in. Pushing back against it, she was overcome by a spirit of despair. Suddenly she felt hopelessness, she felt like there was nothing she could do. But something inside her was pushing back. Something was telling her to let loose, to own her place, what she was.

Think, dammit think! How do I take over this monster? What would make it respond? She was the beast master! It will have to listen. But how?

Another wave of despair fell over her.

What's the point? She could feel the water around her mouth, itching to get intimate, to rush down into her lungs. Panic started to overtake. *I was hasty thinking that I could just bring a dragon into the issue. Austerley was nuts. Trying to take on this sort of thing, this sort of evil. The blackness reached deep into her brain, and she feared her mind was overcome. She was a failure. Just like her mother. Her mother had obviously not lasted the pace and neither had she.*

And all for what? I've never had a real man in my life, no family, there's no career. No aspirations, I've achieved nothing. And as for this fantasy right here, what's the point of it. I'm going to be dead.

She reached out with a hand, and it caught the cloak. *Another piece of vanity.* Then her hand slid to her breastbone and caught a chain. She touched the cross that Kirkgordon had put on her. *And where have you been? All those years in chapel sitting there, listening, singing politely, where have you been? Look at Kirkgordon, a mess, another fallen on your false hopes. And how many more?*

And a voice came in her head. "Lift me up." *What? What on earth is that meant to mean? Sing hymns and stuff beneath the water?* "Lift me up." *How do I do that? Where are you?* "Lift me up."

Her hand clutched around the cross as her mind raced, her last desperate thoughts.

Some literature about creatures, intelligent creatures, not so intelligent creatures, what was it? Who had said it? She couldn't remember. "Lift me up." *The dragon, so easy to talk to, to communicate with, a full discussion. This mind, this mind of evil, there's nothing, no conversation.*

Not the higher functions, just basic functions, tap into the basic function. Not a man, not reasoning, not controlling, just tapping into the basic function. Desperately her mind raced to know what that was. *Tentacles, tentacles, they have tentacles. What do any tentacles look to do? Unfurl, lift up and lift off.* Scarlett let her mind stretch out, giving everything inside her, what would have been a full wild yell if she had been using a vocal chords. *Lift up! Unfurl! Lift up, unfurl!*

She clung her arms around the dragon's neck as they started to move, the water around her rushing past. They were moving up, up to the surface! Only, she hoped it was up, her orientation not as reliable as when she had first hit the water. Suddenly, air was around her face, and she was spluttering, coughing and spluttering. The dragon was also shaking its head, spitting out water from its throat. And she knew it wasn't finished.

Unfurl, unfurl!

She grabbed the dragons mind and felt its relief as the grip on it released, and they were flying upward in the air. But everything was groggy. *Wings, flap our damn wings!* The creature was motionless until its wings partially spread out. They didn't flap but barely moved, and Scarlett thought they were going to drop back into the ocean. But instead, they landed hard in the middle of the tanker, and she dropped from her position on the dragon's neck. She didn't have time to look as the dragon fell through the outer cover into the hold beneath. The sheer weight of the dragon tore down into the hold, and looking through the dragons eyes she saw a black liquid spraying there. *Diesel!*

Everything was pain with the dragon, and she knew she had her own limbs that were screaming at her. But she needed to get her creature back up from the hold below. Looking back through the dragon's eyes, she saw the inner of the hold empty but filling now with a black liquid. The dragon hurt from its wings to its feet, every limb aching, but it pushed its way out through the hole above. Several men that had gathered at the edge were knocked aside as the dragon fought back through it. But it could not maintain its strength and merely collapsed onto the top of the tanker and lay there, desperately breathing, struggling to move.

Scarlett broke off from the dragon's mind and quickly looked around her. Black tentacles were coming up through the sea and a large number of men with strange heads were looking over the edge of the tanker at what must have been the Kraken breaking through the waves. Then she saw the man coming towards her to take hold of her. The dragon was motionless, and she wondered what to do now that her main weapon was gone. She sought briefly to reach back to the Kraken but the mind was too strong, and she wasn't close enough even if she could work out what to do anyway. There was no point trying to tell it to do things too complicated beyond a simple motion of its body. She waited for the men to grab her.

One of the men was lifted off his feet, having been hit in the shoulder. Another crossbow bolt struck a second man, and he went down, while from behind her, someone jumped over and ran into the crowd ahead of her. Scarlett saw Kirkgordon's flailing arm floor a man with one hit before sweeping another off his feet. He threw something into a man ten feet away before firing a crossbow bolt into another man further away.

"Go back the way I came," he shouted. "Austerley's up there. Go back the way I came. There's a corner up there I can defend you."

Scarlett didn't wait for any further invitation but turned and ran, cloak billowing out behind. She saw Austerley in the doorway of a small structure. As he was approached by several of the strange headed men, she marvelled at how he first created something in the air. It was some sort of hole which a couple of them were dragged into and then seemed to disappear. But one reached Austerley and his head was driven into the steel structure causing him to fall to the ground, blood pouring from his nose. Scarlett screamed.

The men turned to her. She didn't know what to do, tried to turn, to run to the other side of the vessel but now more men appeared. And then they began falling to the ground, bolts stuck in their bodies. From behind them, a figure appeared grabbing her hand and running towards Austerley. Scarlett found herself being taken and told to stand behind Austerley whilst Kirkgordon stood in front of them taking on all comers. He was so fluid with his motions, moving here and there.

"I've hit the panic button, but I don't think they're coming," said Kirkgordon.

Scarlett had no idea what he was on about. *What panic button?* She wasn't able to ask as he ducked this way and that before being dropped to the floor by an unseen punch. Austerley was out cold on the floor, not moving. Maybe he was dead? Scarlett began to shake, and she reached out to the dragon but all she got back was *move!* And then she saw him.

It was like a dark image that slid across the vessel but she knew what was coming. It seemed like a man that wasn't entirely there. She watched as Kirkgordon was unable to swing his arm into the shadow then he collapsed to the floor. He was motionless, totally motionless. Tears began to well up in Scarlett's eyes as she realised she was alone.

"Yes, your mother was like this at the end, yes."

Something that felt like a hand reached out across her face. She looked up into darkness. There were seemingly no eyes, just something hollow, something black in the face. She struggled to distinguish anything about the man except for the foreboding that was assaulting her.

"As beautiful as your mother," said the shadow man and his hand ran across her face, then to her neck and then settled on her breastbone. "And missing something. Your mother couldn't do it properly without the necklace. She could do the party tricks, the little animals, but the creatures, never without the necklace. You spoke to a Kraken, you spoke to evil. Just beautiful."

Scarlett shivered as the hand ran across her body from the front to hips and down her legs. It wasn't the touch of a lover looking at your body, wasn't even like some sort of lecherous pest. This was different. This was almost like being a prized pet.

"You're thinking I look at you like a freak," said the shadow man, "and I do. You are a freak, a beautiful freak. Differently constructed. Not the norm. Scary to those around you, don't you think? You only feel normal because of these freaks around you. The fat man who can do things from nothing, and the fighter with his funny arm. Just freaks like you. I was sorry when I had to kill your mother, but she wouldn't stop. She kept resisting instead of becoming my slave. I think you will become my slave, I think you're afraid today."

Scarlett reached up to her breastbone.

"I see you replaced it. Did someone give you that or did you buy that, yourself? Cheap trinkets, the trinket of my enemy.

The master won't let his slave wear something like that."

Scarlett felt a hand over hers which tried to pull at the necklace, tried to pull her hand away, seeking to rip it off her neck. Then a thought came to her. *Freak or no freak, I'm made perfectly. That's what they always said back then, each one of us was made perfectly the way we were meant to be. I am a freak.*

"I will be no slave," declared Scarlett. "Kill me, or whatever, but I will be no slave."

She closed her eyes and heard the shadow man talk on but she wasn't listening. Feeling his hand running back up the side of the body, she ignored it, choosing to reach out with her mind to her dragon.

One last time, just one last time onto your feet.

Yes master, one last time.

So the dragon slowly, limply, started to get up. There was no one around it. Seemingly, they had presumed it was dead.

Time to head back to the hole you created in the tanker. Some fire, some fire, my lovely, some fire for Scarlett. The dragon's neck moved back in a slightly customary fashion before letting rip a ball of fire into the hold. The hole produced heavy orange flames into the air, coupled with black smoke, as the diesel ignited. From within the hold came an explosion which rocked the vessel and everyone on deck started to lose their feet. The shadow man too, fell away

"What are you doing? Why resist?"

Scarlett laughed. "Can you swim? You travel across surfaces; you seem to linger to surfaces. Can you linger on the water?" She laughed again. When all hope was gone, she had only one hope to trust. Placed in the one they said had made her, the one she had been distant from but the one who made her to be that person she was made to be. Her hand still clutched the cross. Kirkgordon was right, in the darkest moment it became a light.

The dragon was still on its feet but that wasn't the direction she needed to go as the boat rocked left and right. The shadow man struggled to grasp her as she turned and ran to the edge of the boat. She hoped and prayed it would continue to rock as she grabbed the side of it, hooking her arms around the barrier, sitting on her backside. *Not the most elegant pose but frankly, who gives a damn.*

With her mind she reached out, felt the blackness, felt the darkness coming at it. Impending doom was within the creature. It was time to embrace it, time to let it do what it does. *Take it. Take the ship. Wrap around it and take it.*

Nothing was happening. Too complicated, far too complicated. Concentrate on a limb, make it wrap, limb by limb. Wrap!

She saw one of the black limbs that sat on the black tentacles coming out and wrapping itself around the vessel. The slick, jet black octopus-like limb tore into the vessel despite the turmoil around. Then another limb sprung up and wrapped. And another. And another one. *Down, take her down!* This was her last play. Scarlett laughed.

"You won't do this." It was the shadow man, and he was moving towards her.

"Yes, I will, and I have won! You killed my friends, destroyed my dragon and you come for my world. Better me, better I die and stop it right here."

"But my master lives on, he's here. He will have your world."

"But you won't get to see that. I hope my mother's watching this and laughing at you!"

The Shadow stepped forward to grab Scarlett, and she felt her hair being pulled. She screamed as another hand went to her shoulder but she clung on, her arms wrapped around the side of the vessel. And then the grip was released, and she watched him disappear off the edge of the boat into the water. She searched, desperate to see what happened, more transfixed than in control. Watching him sink into the water, she realised he couldn't swim. He couldn't swim.

Scarlett turned round on hearing a gruff shout.

"We need to get off, we need to get off this thing. That bloody creature's taking it into the sea."

"I know, I told it to take it down."

"But we're still on board!"

"Yes, but it will take it, it will mean the Kraken will go back. The Kraken will go back to the deep. Austerley wasn't here to oblige." She smiled a forlorn smile, sad to leave the world but happy in her decision.

"Your dragon? Can it fly?" asked Kirkgordon.

"It's injured. Besides I'm taking the Kraken to the deep, I'm controlling it."

"Trust me, it's going to the deep, and so are we. It's doing what comes naturally. Get your dragon to fly!"

As if on dramatic cue, the vessel started to tilt. It was ablaze and now the centre was bending towards the sea, driving both ends up into the air. Scarlett was still hanging on to the edge at some railings but Kirkgordon immediately fell and tumbled down towards the sea which was engulfing the centre of the vessel.

"No!" she screamed but then had the presence of mind to realise that she couldn't do anything, not without her beast.

Get up!

I can't.

Get up! There was pain, there was anguish, there was despair but she reached out and made those wings move. *We need to fly, we need to fly.* The vessel was tilting, and she reached for the claws of the dragon to hold it on the vessel before it tumbled to the sea. Both ends of the ship were starting to roll up, and she feared soon her own body would have to fall off. The wings beat. In pain, but they beat, and lifted the dragon's weight off the vessel. It rose to the air and turned and circled up towards one end of the vessel that had tilted.

Scanning the deck, she saw Austerley's body through the dragon's eyes and saw it was beginning to tumble down to the sea. A claw reached down and grabbed him, and the dragon wheeled haphazardly towards Scarlett. Letting go, she grabbed herself with the other claw. Seeing herself through its eyes was surreal but she focused on the matter in hand and scanned the sea looking for Kirkgordon.

But then she felt something wrap around the claw. It was tight, just above with the talons and looking down from the dragon's eye, she saw a rope. Hanging from that rope by means of his false arm was Kirkgordon. *Go, go!* The dragon flapped its wings as hard as it could. Behind, the ship was moving further into the water, either end now completely risen toward the sky and meeting at the top. The Kraken pulled its victim down, deep into the sea.

Scarlett used the dragon to look desperately for the land it had seen before, a small island. It was in pain, she could feel it, but she kept it pushing its wings as the dragon flew low, struggling to gain any height. When the land came into view, she could feel the dragon's relief, descending on the island and releasing its cargo onto the sand. Scarlett flopped onto the beach, then cleared from the dragon's mind. Looking out to sea, she saw where Kirkgordon had splashed down when released. He was swimming with one arm. After five minutes, he emerged from the surf and sat down beside her. He was soaking wet, his face was caked in blood and his arm was simply open with a crossbow still hanging out of it.

"Well done," said Kirkgordon, "Bloody well done!"

"Just another freak," said Scarlett, "Just me, the freak."

"We're all freaks," said Kirkgordon, "I realised that a long time ago. But don't tell Austerley, he's still the chief freak."

Scarlett laughed, then laid back before falling asleep. She didn't wake until the sun's rays had warmed her. The world was good, she was on an island beach with a dragon, a cultist and a man with a mechanical arm laid open and showing a weapon. Her life was okay, almost fun.

21

A Freak's Place in the World

Lying in the bath, she felt the water soak into her bones. She was tired. No, not just tired, she was weary after this weird odyssey. It seemed like she had just been falling from one thing to another, never having time to really stop and process. She struggled to comprehend all that had happened. Wilson was in a mess. Calandra was badly hurt, and just when she had thought the woman was almost indestructible. And then there was the Kraken. Watching the boys almost succumb before they were able to turn things around. Austerley had been out cold and useless, and yet she had thought of him as the powerful one, the person who truly knew things.

There came a buzz at her door and now that the quiet was broken, she stepped out of the bath. Reaching for a white robe, she caught a glimpse of herself in the mirror and then turned to examine herself fully. Was she more toned, she wondered, from all this exertion? Maybe. But the scar was still there. Reaching a hand up to her breastbone, she felt along the charred flesh. They offered surgery, but she had rejected it. It reminded her that she didn't need it. She had talked to, controlled, no, influenced the Kraken without it. But she was now paying the price. Bad thoughts and evil murmurings were there in her mind. Haunted, they had said. They were right.

There was a tap at the door, reminding her that someone was waiting for her. Wrapping her white robe around herself, Scarlett exited the bathroom into a small bedroom and lounge. Opening the door to her quarters, she saw Calandra. The woman was, as usual, dressed like some fashionable mercenary with her long black boots, black leather trousers and black crop top, although the jacket was missing. Instead of wholly bare arms, she was wearing long gloves. Calandra entered without a word and passed by to the window, looking out to the Scottish hills and fields beyond.

"How you doing?" asked Calandra, without looking back at Scarlett.

"Tired," Scarlett answered. "Definitely tired."

"Felt that before. Definitely felt that before." The woman stood in silence contemplating the land through the window, and Scarlett wasn't sure what to do. *Well, let's try the old tried and trusted.* Putting the kettle on, Scarlett dropped a couple of teabags into the teapot. This base, this place, was funny. The whole place was funny. Here they were running around doing all this chasing of strange creatures, taking on impossible situations, yet here in her room the teapot has a view of the valleys on it and sat beside it were a couple of bags of Welsh tea. Little touches like that. Probably Wilson's doing.

"Thank you," said Calandra.

"Thank me. What for?"

"For saving me, thank you for saving me. I doubt I would

have made it. How's the bird?"

"He's all right. He went back to the zoo for a while but he's coming back. He's restless up there, seems to be restless without me, bursting into flame. They are recommending he comes back here to me."

"And thank you for saving the boys," said Calandra. "For saving him."

"Okay," said Scarlett, "it wasn't like it was deliberate. Everybody was kind of looking after my backside at the same time. Just desperate to survive. To be fair, it was my first Kraken. He seemed more adept with these creatures, I was more cumbersome."

"Give it time." Calandra continued to look out of the window, but she was shaking, her head was slightly off kilter. "I need to be sharper. It's hard, but it's good to know he's okay. Thank you."

"What's the problem? Why don't you guys just get it together?"

"His wife. It's a bit of an issue."

"But if he wants you more than her, why doesn't he…?"

"Don't go there! She's a gibbering wreck because of me. When it came time to choose, he chose me and I burned him, nearly lost his arms. And now she's a gibbering wreck, lost in a dark mind. He's better off without me. Why do you think I'm here with you?"

Scarlett knew this wasn't a good place to go, so she merely began to pour the tea. Tapping Calandra's shoulder, she handed her the now warm vessel. There came another knock at the door.

On opening the door, Scarlett saw Wilson in a wheelchair with Rodriguez behind him. *Look at Wilson, he's got a leg in plaster, bandages on his sides and arms, and yet he's still looking dapper, complete with that bowler hat. You can't keep these people down.*

"I must say, you've done rather well," said Wilson, "done rather well, Miss. Indeed, for a rookie, you've even excelled yourself. But you must realise that the job isn't done."

"The job? What job? I came here, I helped. I put that Kraken back to rest."

"Yes, an excellent job, but now there is the demon to consider, it's loose. And there are more creatures. It will look to build an army unless we can stop it. So I need you."

"A request?" asked Scarlett.

"Had I the luxury of making a request, then I would make it. This is a demand. Your country needs you. In fact, the world does, to be frank. These challenges that come up in my Department are not run-of-the-mill matters. To deal with them, I need all of the talented individuals I can get. Mr. Rodriguez here is at my disposal and very helpful despite his diminutive size. Miss Calandra, despite all the wounds she carries over all these years, is still my best fighter with a coolness that strikes fear into many. Then there's people like me, resourceful, keeping things going."

"A quick review, Wilson, everyone gets hurt. I doubt I'll last long."

"There is that," nodded Wilson, "But we're not in a James Bond novel here. Understand that if you don't stay with us, you'll find yourself alone dealing with these things. The trouble with people like us is that the dark is drawn to us. They see the challenge, see someone who wants to stop them. I'd love to let you run back to your former life, but as I said, I don't have that luxury. I'm not here to make a request, I'm here to set you up for your next mission."

"Next mission?" said Scarlett, "Where would that be?"

"As I said, the demon still exists and is hiding low somewhere. You need to find him. I had to send the boys off on another errand, but as soon as they are finished, I can get them back to help you. They shouldn't be gone long. In the meantime, you are going to have to hunt the demon down. As for myself, as you can see, I'm going take a little while to be back at full steam."

Scarlett lifted her hand up to her neck and felt the deep scar. Yes, she was part of this now. Turning her back to Wilson, she walked over to the window and stood beside Calandra, gazing out at the hills with patches of snow on their tops.

"You can't go back," said Calandra. "When these things happen you can't go back. When I was changed hundreds of years ago, it took me several lifetimes to find my home. Even then I almost lost it. I almost lost him. You need to look around you, because this is family, weird and bizarre, but family. You're a freak like us, so you might as well be amongst freaks."

Scarlett nodded. She remembered being that loser woman who the boys only wanted for parts of her body. Countless boring dates, time spent with men who didn't really care. Doing a job that was just monotonous. But now, she had a dragon in South America. There was a firebird coming to sit on her shoulder. She knew a man who could tell how to wreak havoc on these creatures of the night. And she could also be someone. Someone classy, yes someone classy.

"Okay," said Scarlett, "I'm in. But only on one condition. Scarlett tilted her head up slightly, looking to Calandra's eyes. "It all depends on you. If we're gonna be partners, you need to help me dress to kill, like you.

A Small Request

Many thanks for taking the time to read "Scarlett O'Meara" and I hope you enjoyed it as much as I did writing the story. As an Indie author, I am constantly seeking to make more people aware of my writing. As such I would ask that if you enjoyed "Scarlett O'Meara: Beastmaster" please leave a review so others will know about the dynamic that is the world of SETAA.

Kind regards,
  Gary

About the Author

GR Jordan is a self-published author who finally decided at forty that in order to have an enjoyable lifestyle, his creative beast within would have to be unleashed. His books mirror that conflict in life where acts of decency contend with self-promotion, goodness stares in horror at evil and kindness blind-side us when we at our worst. Corrupting our world with his parade of wondrous and horrific characters, he highlights everyday tensions with fresh eyes whilst taking his methodical, intelligent mainstays on a roller-coaster ride of dilemmas, all the while suffering the banter of their provocative sidekicks.

A graduate of Loughborough University where he masquer-aded as a chemical engineer but ultimately played American football, Gary had worked at changing the shape of cereal flakes and pulled a pallet truck for a living. Watching vegetables freeze at -40'C was another career highlight and he was also one of the Scottish Highlands "blind" air traffic controllers. These days he has graduated to answering a telephone to people in trouble before telephoning other people to sort it out.

Having flirted with most places in the UK, he is now based in the Isle of Lewis in Scotland where his free time is spent between raising a young family with his wife, writing, figuring out how to work a loom and caring for a small flock of chickens. Luckily his writing is influenced by his varied work and life experience as the chickens have not been the poetical inspiration he had hoped for!

You can connect with me on:
- http://www.grjordan.com
- http://www.twitter.com/carpetless
- http://www.facebook.com/carpetlessleprechaun
- https://www.amazon.com/G-R-Jordan/e/B00P6WP9FS/

Subscribe to my newsletter:
- http://grjordan.com/download-footsteps

Also by G R Jordan

G R Jordan writes fantasy books in several series, including the Austerley & Kirkgordon series which spawned the novel you have just read. At the time of publishing, he has produced 6 novels and 3 origin novelettes as well as appearing in anthologies. For a darker read, try "The Blasphemous Welcome", the first book in his "Dark Wen" series.

Crescendo! An Austerley & Kirkgordon Adventure #1
https://www.books2read.com/ak1
A shape-shifting dragon. A cult bringing forth a nightmare. Two broken men, separated by hatred, must bind together to save the world.

Bitter-sweet partners, Austerley and Kirkgordon, take on the darkness to prevent a displaced people ending the world. If you like bizarre creatures, fast paced action and cataclysmic nightmares, you'll love G R Jordan's first novel. Get the book readers have called " a fast paced gothic thriller with lots of humour" and "refreshingly modern take on Lovecraftian themes."

Can the Elder darkness be stopped? It's the blasphemous fanfare for the end of the world!

The Darkness at Dillingham: An Austerley & Kirkgordon Adventure #2
https://www.books2read.com/ak2
An exhibitionist witch. A English seaside town literally descending to hell. And the only hope is a broken partnership that doesn't want to heal!

"The Darkness at Dillingham" is the second instalment in the A&K urban fantasy series. If you like breakneck action, sexy villains and cutting dialogue, then you'll love this misfit set of heroes. Can the team bind together long enough to rescue a cursed town? Get the book one reader called "A real roller coaster of spookiness with some sexy bits thrown in".

Dillingham, the nightlife's straight from hell!

Dagon's Revenge: An Austerley & Kirkgordon Adventure #3

https://www.books2read.com/ak3

A shattered hero races to save his wife. A rescue team falling apart. Elder god Dagon's coming back and he's pissed!

Kirkgordon takes his team beyond our world in this third instalment in the Austerley & Kirkgordon urban fantasy series. If you like danger and desire, punchy dialogue and cataclysmic nightmares then you'll love G R Jordan's bunch of discombobulated heroes.

Sometimes, there are no good choices!

Footsteps: Austerley & Kirkgordon Origins #1

https://www.books2read.com/akorigins1

An insane professor. A journey into a New England grave. Will Kirkgordon return alive?

It was supposed to be a quiet protection job. But under a New England grave yard Kirkgordon meets his worst nightmares. Will he make it out alive with his protectee? Or will he kill him, himself?

Kirkgordon gets his first taste of dark creatures in this first origin story from the A&K universe. If like you like action and adventure, dark creatures from beyond and cutting dialogue from antagonistic heroes then you'll love G R Jordan's A&K urban fantasy series.

Is the real madness above or below the surface?

Cally: Austerley & Kirkgordon Origins #2

https://www.books2read.com/akorigins2

A village emptied of its children. A warrior finding her greatest desire. But a witch's vengeance wrecks a curse that will devastate her forever.

The tale of Calandra's curse is the 2nd story in the A&K origins series, a collection of short stories that expand G R Jordan's A&K universe. If you love rollicking action, imperfect heroes and extraordinary, magical villains, then you will love the Austerley & Kirkgordon series.

Yesterday, he offered her the rest of his life. Today a vengeful witch wants to take him away. Can Calandra's dreams survive the mother of all storms?

Sometimes a woman can be too cold for any man!

The People in the Pool: Austerley & Kirkgordon Origins #3

https://www.books2read.com/akorigins3

He lost her, murdered a long time ago. But now she's returned. If something isn't real, does it matter?

"The People in the Pool" is the 3rd origin story in the A&K origins series, a collection of short stories that expand G R Jordan's A&K universe. If you love rollicking action, imperfect heroes and weird villains and places, then you will love the Austerley & Kirkgordon series.

Not every mother can warm a child's heart.

The Blasphemous Welcome: Dark Wen Book # 1

https:www.books2read.com/dw1

A demonic entity prepares a bloody path for its master. Four fiendish ways for the city folk to die. A cynical, battle weary detective must become his home's heavenly protector.

Join Detective Trimble and fresh faced Kyla Corstain as they enter a world of evil and ungodly manipulation causing murder, mayhem and disaster. The war for a city's soul begins now!

The Dark Wen series opens with a fanfare of destruction and death raining upon a city held in the grip of an unknown force. If you like dark powers, fast paced action and a generous dose of occult warfare, then "The Blasphemous Welcome" will satisfy your story cravings.

An explosive hello to evil incarnate!